A Bride for the Viscount's Cold Son

A Regency Romance Novel

Audrey Ashwood

ISBN: 9781793002525
Imprint: Independently published

About this Novel

A poor village orphan.
An unexpected fortune.
Can she overcome her humble beginnings to find true love?

Regency London. Lavinia Talridge is heartbroken. After the premature death of her mother, young Lavinia is left destitute, with no money and no family.

Until, in a twist of fate, she discovers that she is wealthy. Before she can believe her new life of privilege is true, Lavinia has an arranged marriage to a handsome gentleman and a chance at love.

But when the Viscount's son acts coldly towards her, Lavinia assumes her lower-class background is to blame. Afraid to go through with the potentially-joyless marriage, can the young woman find a lifetime worth of love?

A Sweet Regency Romance with a dash of suspense. If you like authentic women, romantic moments, and surprising fortunes, then you'll love this delightful love story.

Chapter 1

The cold air seeped under the door, and through every crack in the walls of the stone cottage. Inside, the fire in the hearth did little to dispel the chill in the corners of the rooms, as the wind howled outside. Lavinia trembled, but it was not from the cold, it was from fear. Her mother lay on a pallet by the fireside, her skin burning hot to the touch.

"Mama, please tell me what to do," Lavinia pleaded as she placed a wet compress on her mother's forehead. "I am frightened. Can you hear me?"

Her mother murmured incoherently, her eyes were closed, her face pale. Lavinia did not know what illness had befallen her mother, but it was terrible in its swiftness. It had begun with a cough, a common enough ailment for winter in Yorkshire. Her cough had not been a source for worry, and neither was the sickness that followed it, nor even the pains that came with her weakened state. For two days, her mother had assured Lavinia that she was suffering only from a slight chill and nothing more. However, by the third day, her mother's condition had become dire, and there was nothing to be done – nothing at all. Over half of the villagers were suffering from this fever, and some of them were dying.

There was no doctor in the village of Cotes Cross, just the local apothecary, but he could do little to ease the suffering of the villagers. He gave advice and prescribed remedies and teas, however, neither

Lavinia nor her mother had more than a few pennies to spare, and pennies would not buy medicine.

"Mama, please drink this, it will feed you," Lavinia begged as she looked at her mother, "You must wake up. How can you drink this broth if you do not wake up?"

Lavinia was frantic. There was no-one to help her and no-one to tell her what to do to save her mother's life. Outside it was dark and the snow was falling heavy and fast. She was left with a terrible choice. Should she leave her mother all alone as she tried to fetch help from a neighbour, or should she remain at her side? If she left, then what if her mother needed her? What if her mother died? She would not be able to live with the guilt, if her mother died alone. However, if she stayed, her mother might die without help. It was a terrible decision and one that she felt powerless to make.

Reaching for her mother's hand, she found it to be limp. There was no strength in her mother's fingers. Lavinia kissed her mother's hand, holding it against her tear-stained face. "Dear Lord, please spare my mother, please do not take her. I beg of you Lord, please hear me."

Her mother's breathing was quiet, growing fainter with every passing moment. Lavinia was overcome with fear and grief as she wept, "Mama, please speak to me. Wake up, wake up! Do not die, you cannot die. What will I do without you?"

The woman lying on the pallet did not speak; she did not wake up. With one terrible convulsion, she moaned, and then after one long breath, she breathed no more.

Lavinia sat on in silence. Her heart's beating inside her chest was so furious that she feared she may die herself. Her mother couldn't be dead; she was too young and too alive. What if she was only sleeping, what if Lavinia was wrong? Peering at her mother's unmoving face, she knew that she was wishing for what could never be. The stiff hand that lay in hers and the lifeless pallor of her mother's skin was evidence of the terrible truth. Lavinia gave herself to her grief and wept as she laid her head on her mother's chest.

From the second that followed her mother's last agonised breath, Lavinia Dean had become a poor, wretched orphan. The only family she had ever known was gone. As the fire in the hearth slowly burned itself out, Lavinia was numb to the cold that overpowered her. At the age of thirteen, she would have to find her own way in the world.

Lavinia was not sure how long she sat at her mother's side. The fire finally went out, and she did not make a move to relight it. One by one, the candles burned away until they were extinguished, leaving only one left burning away the gloom. The wind howled through the chimney as she held her mother's cold hand in her own until the dawn. She was not aware that she was shivering, or that her teeth were chattering.

As she mourned her mother's passing, she was also gripped by a terrible uncertainty. How would she survive? How would she buy food to eat? She did not know what was to become of her. What became of orphans? Would she be forced to live on the streets of the village, begging for scraps to eat? Her young mind could not conceive of a worse horror. Witnessing the death of her mother was a tragedy, but she was terrified of what else might befall her. It was far too terrible to consider. Gripped by sorrow and fear, she lay down next to her mother and cried herself into a fitful sleep.

In the light of day, Lavinia stared at her mother's face. Her mother was so beautiful in life, her laugh so cheerful. Yet it was her singing that Lavinia thought about as she sat in silent vigil. Her mother was timid in church but in her cottage, or in the yard, she would sing as sweetly as the birds in spring. She sang hymns and ballads that would make Lavinia cry. Of all the songs her mother sang, it was the old tunes about love that Lavinia cherished. She would never hear her mother's voice raised in song again; never hear her laugh. She would never feel her mother's warm embrace. Lavinia was not aware that she was weeping; her feelings were in turmoil as she tried to accept the loss of her mother.

She was curled up at her mother's side, when a kind neighbour found her later that day. Mrs Derring, the wife of the local thatcher, discovered Lavinia in her pitiful state. The young girl was wracked with cold when she was taken from her cottage. The thatcher's wife was a good woman who did not have much money to spend on her own family, let alone Lavinia. In the winter there was not much thatching work, nor was there much money until the work returned in the spring. While lacking in wealth, she nevertheless possessed a generous nature. In her snug cottage, there was a warm sitting room, a narrow trundle bed and thin but plentiful stew.

Lavinia did not recall the early hours she spent in the thatcher's cottage, with his wife and their six children. She barely remembered the thatcher arguing with his wife, fearful that Lavinia was sick with the same illness that had killed her mother. She heard the sound of fear in the man's voice, but she did not know if that was a fantasy or if it was real. Falling in and out of sleep, she finally woke from her fitful dreams, on the night following her mother's death. She found Mrs Derring at the fireside. Lavinia ate the meagre stew offered to her, even though she did not have an appetite. Mrs Derring was a tender-hearted woman, and in her grief-torn state, Lavinia did not want to offend her.

She did not leave the generous hospitality of the thatcher's cottage until the day of the funeral. As she stood at the graveside, with snow up to her ankles, she hardly knew how her mother came to be placed in the wooden box by the open grave. The vicar gave his eulogy of her mother, saying a few words about her mother's industriousness and the untimeliness of her death. Lavinia saw her neighbours say their goodbyes. She watched silently as her mother's plain coffin was lowered into the ground of the churchyard. She stood at her mother's graveside until her feet were numb.

Lavinia had attracted the attention of the vicar, as she shivered in the churchyard. Father Harding was an elderly man, who to her young eyes looked to be a hundred years old. With his hunched back and thin wooden cane, he moved slowly and carefully towards her, until he was close enough to see her breath hanging in the freezing January air.

"My dear, you cannot stay out here. You'll take ill," he said as he put his thin hand on her shoulder. "Come inside the rectory, sit by the fire."

Lavinia nodded her head, following him back to the modest stone cottage beside the village church. A short, plump woman, who was the vicar's wife, greeted Lavinia at the door, "My lamb, you'll catch your death standing out in the snow. Come inside and warm yourself in the sitting room."

Lavinia did as she was told. Her fingers tingled as if pins and needles were stabbing them through her thin gloves, as the feeling returned to them.

Looking down at her boots, she realised they were soaked.

The plump woman pulled out a wooden chair by the hearth for Lavinia, "Sit down... you look like you might fall over. Sit, I will bring you a cup of tea."

Lavinia sat on the chair, aware that the vicar was staring at her. Looking at him, she did not say anything as she had been taught not to speak first to her elders.

"I am sorry for your loss. Your mother was a good woman, and I often thought her talent was wasted in a village of this size. She was one of the best plain-sewing women I ever met."

"Thank you," Lavinia whispered, looking down at her hands.

"I do not remember your mother speaking to me about her family. Do you have any aunts or uncles?"

"No sir, I do not. It was just me and Mama."

"What about your father? Is there any family on his side who might take you in?"

"No sir," she answered, feeling very alone, despite the kindness of the vicar and his wife.

She glanced at the vicar; his old, gnarled face was twisted into a stern expression. He rubbed his chin as he studied her before he spoke, "Have faith, my dear, that the Lord will see you through this time of trial."

Lavinia did not know about the Lord seeing her through. She hoped with all her might that the Lord would show her mercy. She was going to need his mercy if she was going to survive.

Chapter 2

Father Harding invited Lavinia to stay at the rectory for a few days, but she declined his offer. Instead, she left with a hamper of food from the vicar's kitchen and a few pennies in her pocket.

The village had always been her home and when she walked along the narrow lanes of Cotes Cross, she realized that she knew every building and every house that crowded the streets. The buildings were old, like the village, and built of grey stone and timber. Today, she felt old too, far older than her years. She also felt alone.

Lavinia could have accepted the kindness of the vicar and the thatcher's or the other friendly villagers who kept inquiring about her well-being, but how could she be a burden to any of these people who had barely enough for themselves? She needed time to sort out the thoughts that were swirling in her head. Her chest hurt from the grief, her face was wet from crying, and her feet and hands were stinging from the cold. She saw the sympathetic looks of the people she passed on the street, as she made her way home to the cottage. Everyone in this small hamlet knew everyone else, and there were no secrets in Cotes Cross. Lavinia could feel the pity emanating from her well-meaning neighbours. One day soon, she might need to rely on that pity to live. Today, she needed to be at home, in the one place that reminded her of her mother.

Opening the wooden door of the cottage, she heard the familiar creak of the hinges. It used to be a welcoming sound when neighbours came to call, bringing their sewing to her mother. For a moment, the creaking hinges brought a smile to her face as she recalled happier times. Then she closed the door behind her and stood alone in the room. The cottage was cold, and the thick walls held the chill of winter. She set the hamper down on the rough-hewn table and gazed at the place on the floor where her mother had died.

The pallet was gone and with it all traces of the tragedy that had stolen her mother away from her. The hearth was swept, and a stack of fresh firewood lay in the fireplace. She did not know who had arranged the funeral, or who had paid for the coffin, but she could feel the generosity of her neighbours. In this tiny village in Yorkshire, her mother's friends were generous to her even in death. This was a moment that would live with Lavinia for a long time.

Sitting beside her own fireside, she noticed her mother's sewing box on the table beside the hamper of food, and a pile of mending sat neatly folded beside it. Lavinia wiped her tears from her eyes and wondered if she might find enough work mending and sewing just as her mother had done. She was strong for her age, despite her tiny frame. She could work; she could do odd jobs to earn money.

Would anyone pay her to do their sewing and mending? She crossed the tiny room and picked up a shirt, holding it up and looking at it. The tiny even stitches were nearly invisible, evidence of her mother's skill with a needle. She thought of what the vicar had said about her mother's talent and questioned whether she could do the same.

Her own sewing skills were coming along, as her mother used to say. She would allow Lavinia to help make mattress ticking or pillow cases, but that was all. Lavinia was not allowed to sew clothes, at least not yet. Her mother had dreams for Lavinia – dreams that she said would come true one day. Her mother prayed that Lavinia would not be a plain-sewing woman; she was not going to do odd jobs around the village to buy food. She was going to be married, her mother had often repeated in a cheerful voice, perhaps to a tradesman, a farmer or even a respected reverend?

How Lavinia wished she shared her mother's hopes... She folded the shirt and placed it back on the pile. What could a girl of her age do in the world? She and her mother had lived plainly. The cottage and its sparse furnishings were all she had ever known, but she knew that other people did not live the way she had. The vicar, for example, and his wife had a nice house; their sitting room contained two uphol-stered chairs and a set of polished candlesticks. Maybe she could find work in a kitchen at a great house?

She thought about working in a manor house, cleaning and polish-ing all day long. The work would be hard, but she would have plenty of food to eat and a bed of her own. But would she want to leave the only place she had ever known? This cottage with these two tiny rooms had been her home since she was a child. Her neighbours had been the only people, aside from her Mama, whom she knew. Their children were her friends and the women were like aunts to her. She hadn't lied to the vicar when he asked her about her family, but she felt a twinge of guilt. She *did* have a family, but they were not related by blood – they were the people of Cotes Cross. If she left the village, she wouldn't know anyone, and no-one would know her. Lavinia had always been a quiet, timid child and the prospect of striking out for herself was nearly as frightening as starving in the streets.

The tears came again as she stared into the fire. The vicar had said to have faith. She had faith, but she did not know if faith was enough to save her.

A loud rapping at the door startled Lavinia so terribly that she jumped. Was it the landlord coming for the rent? *I should have stayed at the vicar's* she thought, as she sat still, too panicked to move. She could pretend she was not home, but the smoke coming out of the chimney told a different story. Maybe she could give him all the money she had and promise to pay the rest in a week or two? Trembling in fear, Lavinia opened the narrow wooden box on the mantle and removed the meagre amount of coins, counting them.

It was not enough.

With her coins gripped tightly in her hand, she walked to the door, praying that God would have mercy on her. Lavinia opened the door and then immediately stepped back, gasping.

A man stood at the door. He was a tall man dressed in a black coat. She had never seen him before.

"Good day, is this the residence of Miss Lavinia Dean?" he asked as he tipped his hat.

Lavinia had never been called 'Miss' before, and she had never had a man tip his hat to her. She did not know what to make of his strange behaviour. Peering past his hulking frame she saw a sight that was even more astonishing. A carriage was parked on the road, a few steps behind the man. The carriage was unlike any she had ever seen. It had a team of four milk-coloured horses and a gilt crest on the door. It looked like the type of carriage that belonged to lords and ladies, when they rode through town.

Lavinia did not know what the carriage or this man was doing at her cottage, but she tried to remember her manners. "I am Lavinia. I do not have much to offer you, but a seat at my fire."

"That is very kind of you, young Miss. I am the coachman. My mistress wishes to see you."

To Lavinia's astonishment, she watched transfixed as the coachman strode to the carriage. He opened the door and then stood straight and tall, as a woman emerged. Like Lavinia, she was short in stature and thin, but that was where the resemblance ended. The woman who stepped down from the carriage was richly attired in a fur-lined coat and a matching bonnet. She was an older woman, but she was handsome. She smiled at Lavinia.

"Lavinia? Can it be?"

Lavinia did not know this woman who reached out for her. With a curtsey, she answered, "Ma'am, won't you come inside?"

"Thank you, but I won't be staying long... and neither will *you*," the woman said as she bustled past Lavinia and headed inside to the fire.

Against the backdrop of the plaster walls, the dirt floor, and the rough wooden furnishings, Lavinia's guest, attired in her deep-blue coat and bonnet, looked as out of place inside the cottage as the carriage did parked outside of it. Lavinia was too surprised by this turn of events to know quite what to do. Who was this woman and why was she here?

The woman stood by the fire, holding her gloved hands over the flames, as she rubbed them, "There is nothing like a good fire on a winter's day, wouldn't you agree?"

"Yes, ma'am. I can make you a cup of tea. I do not have much, but I do have some bread."

"That won't be necessary," the woman said as she turned around to face Lavinia, "Come and sit down beside me – we have much to discuss."

"We do?" Lavinia asked as she sat on a low wooden stool, leaving the good chair for her guest.

"We do, my girl. Let me have a look at you," the older woman said as she leaned close to Lavinia. She touched Lavinia's chin and gently turned her face one way and then the next, peering closely at her. Lavinia was not sure why she was being studied, but she almost expected the woman to ask her to open her mouth, so she could see her teeth, like a plough horse at the market.

"You have my petite frame and my fine features. Those cheekbones you inherited from my son. Let me see... your hair is as dark as a raven, and you have dark eyes – you must have got those from your mother... she was a beauty," the woman said as she held one of Lavinia's hands. "Your skin is fair. I see your mother did a good job of keeping you out of the sun – splendid."

Lavinia did not intend to be rude, but she was confused, "Ma'am, I do not mean to be impertinent, but I do not know whom I am addressing?"

"My poor dear Lavinia, you do not know me? I am your grandmother. I am Mrs Henrietta Talridge, but you may call me whatever pleases you."

"Grandmother?" Lavinia mouthed the word, unable to speak for a moment. Swallowing, she found her voice again, "I haven't a grandmother. I have no family."

"You do have family, my girl. You have *me*. Your father, God rest his soul, was my son, my only son. You are a Talridge, my dear."

"No, there must be some mistake – my name is Dean."

"Your mother's name was Dean. If you like you may keep it, but to me, you shall be a Talridge. You are all I have left of my dear son; you and I are family."

Lavinia was overwhelmed by the news, and she slowly stood up. She needed a few minutes to collect her thoughts and to make sense of these events. She walked away from the fireside and paced the floor in the confined space.

She sighed. *This is impossible.*

"Forgive my rudeness, but this cannot be true. My mother told me my father was dead and that I had no-one but her," Lavinia replied, her voice cracking from the emotion she could barely conceal.

"My dear, why should you believe me? Here I am a woman you do not know, who has burst in on you at this terrible time of grief. You've been through so much. Sit down, and I will tell you the truth."

Lavinia sat down on her wooden stool beside the fire. She did not know what the truth was, but if there was even the slightest possibility that she may not be alone in the world, she was willing to hear it.

"How old are you?"

"I am not yet fourteen."

"You are practically a woman... Has it really been so long ago? Let me see, where should I start? I know; I will begin with my son, your father. As I have said, he was my only child. He was a handsome man, and he enjoyed a good book and hunting. Your mother was the daughter of a couple who tended the sheep and cattle on my estate. She was a beauty, but you know that, don't you, my dear? My son fell in love with her, but they kept their love secret... I did not know about it. Yes, they kept their love hidden. I suppose he would have thought me too old-fashioned to accept a woman with no connections or family background as a wife, and I am ashamed to say he was right. I wanted my son to marry a woman who was accomplished in all things a lady ought to be. I wanted him to find a wife who could manage the household, entertain guests, and play music. I was blinded by my own ambitions for my son. I did not see... that he showed no interest in any of the eligible young women he met when we went to London for the season."

"You said my mother's parents lived on your estate... are they still alive?" Lavinia wanted to know.

Mrs Talridge shook her head slowly, "No my dear, they died a long time ago, I am sorry to say. They were a good sort of people, hardworking and useful. You would have been proud to know them. They raised your mother to be the same, to work hard for her living."

"And... If you do not mind me asking... was your son in love with my mother?"

"Yes, my son, your father, was in love with your mother. When we returned from London, he made secret plans to marry her. They decided to be wed at the end of the summer, but he, bless his soul, was killed crossing a stream, before they could marry. He was riding his favourite steed, an enormous chestnut if I remember correctly. My poor son fell from the saddle and broke his neck. He died instantly." the old woman said as she reached into the silken purse hanging from her wrist. Retrieving an embroidered handkerchief, she dabbed at her eyes.

"He did not suffer, did he?"

"No, my dear, he did not. I was overcome with grief, however... my husband, your grandfather, had died the year before. When I lost my son, it was more than I could bear. I retreated into a world of grief and despair. I did not want to eat or to leave my room in the morning. For many months, I was inconsolable. It was not until my maid brought me the news that a baby had been born on the estate... a baby that was born out of wedlock, that I had the slightest interest in anything or anyone. At first, I was shocked by the scandal. Who would have been so blatant in their sin to have a baby without the benefit of marriage? I discovered that it was your mother who had given birth... I went to see her that day. It was then that I discovered that my son had been in love with her and that they were planning to be wed. When she told me the news, I did not believe it, but her parents were insistent. They had never lied to me before, so I had no reason to doubt them. As I listened to their story, fantastic as it was, I recalled details about my son that suggested that they were telling the truth..." she looked deep into Lavinia's eyes. "When I held you in my arms, I knew that you were my granddaughter. I felt it in my heart."

"Why have I never met you?" Lavinia asked curiously.

"I do not wish to speak ill of the dead, but that is the fault of your mother, as equally as it is my own. I wanted to have a hand in raising you. I couldn't acknowledge you, of course. You were born out of wedlock... but I had plans for you. When you were of age, I was going to send you to school and give you an education, but your mother did not wish for me to interfere. You were her daughter and the only piece of my son that she had left. Oh, we fought about you bitterly! When she refused to accept my help, I threatened to take you away. Your mother left soon after that, and I did not see her again for many months. By then, she had been living on her own and making her own way in the world. She agreed to take money for your clothes and food, to keep you safe and warm, but she would not take a penny more. I promised I would respect her wishes. I would let her raise you but that when you were older and could make your own choices I would send for you."

"I was born out of wedlock? My mother and father weren't married? That's not true, it cannot be. She told me she was married, and that my father died when I was a baby," Lavinia gasped.

"We won't tell anyone... No-one needs to know. They were going to be married and they had made plans to be wed. He intended to marry her; it was his wish. I decided long ago that when you were older, I would acknowledge you, and I would call you my granddaughter. I should have done it already... but my pride, my terrible pride, stood in the way."

Lavinia reached for the poker and stirred the embers of the dying fire. This morning, she had known who she was. This morning, she was Lavinia Dean, the daughter of a widowed seamstress. Now, she was Lavinia Dean, the granddaughter of a wealthy woman, who was seated across from her at the fireside, and she had been born out of wedlock. The shame of her birth crashed down on her as terribly as the grief she had felt at her mother's passing. She was nobody, and she was a child of sin.

"Let the fire die. We have a long journey to be home in time for dinner," Mrs Talridge said as she stood up.

"*This* is my home," Lavinia answered.

"Not anymore. You are my granddaughter and you're coming with me."

"But... but... I do not want to leave Cotes Cross," Lavinia said, in a panic.

"You can return any time you like, my dear child. Come on, do not tarry. Gather your things," her grandmother rushed.

Lavinia understood that if she left, she would be leaving the only home, she had ever known. The last connection to her mother would be severed when she walked out the door. As badly as it pained her to leave the small cottage, she knew that she did not have a choice, so she slowly packed her clothes into a plain satchel. Before she said goodbye to the cottage, she also packed the wooden box from the mantle, a china case from her mother's bedside table, and her sewing box.

She was in agony as she closed the door for the last time. She did not want to forget her mother, nor the years they had spent in the little house. She vowed that she would never forget the happy memories of her mother singing to her as she sewed.

With fear in her heart, Lavinia sang a verse of her mother's favourite hymn, as she left the cottage forever.

Chapter 3

"Lavinia, do hurry, you do not want to be late for dinner!" the vivacious blond woman called out from the doorway of Lavinia's bedroom.

"Charlotte, what am I to do? I can barely breathe!" Lavinia said as she leaned back against the chair of her vanity.

"You are going to go downstairs to that drawing room and do what we have practiced. You will greet the guests as you always do and enquire about some bland but pleasant topic, such as their health. You will then smile, look demure, and accept any compliments, while your grandmother plans your wedding. There, that is what you shall do."

"Wedding? I am too young to be married... I am not yet nineteen," Lavinia said as she examined her reflection in the mirror.

"My mother was married at eighteen. Loads of proper young ladies are married at your age. It is perfectly acceptable."

"I know it is, but what if I do not like the gentleman? What if he does not like *me*?"

"Lavinia, look at yourself. You are one of the handsomest women in all of Yorkshire. Any man would swoon at the sight of you."

"Charlotte!" Lavinia could not help but smile. "How you lie to me. Is it because my grandmother pays you to flatter me? Is that the reason?"

"I was once your governess, that's true, but now I am your companion. Yes, your grandmother pays me, but even if she did not, I would still call you beautiful. Why would I lie to my friend?"

"Because you feel terribly sorry for me. I haven't your natural grace, nor your fair hair and rosy cheeks."

Charlotte peered into the mirror and adjusted the bow in her hair. "Lavinia, it does not matter what I look like compared to you. You are charming, and you have a loving soul; also, let's not forget that you have a dowry and an annuity. I have my wits and your grandmother's good graces. Who would make a better choice for a wife?"

"Do you think it is my dowry that will make a man want to marry me? Oh, how I wish I could be loved for *me*."

Charlotte smiled. "Lavinia, if you stay locked in your room, you will never know if any man wants to marry you for your money or for love. Stop dawdling about and come with me, before your grandmother comes searching for us. You do not want to make her cross, do you?"

Lavinia shook her head. Her grandmother was a sweet woman, but she was determined and fiercely independent. When she was cross, she could be a tyrant. With one last look in the mirror, Lavinia sighed. She saw her mother's dark hair curled and swept into a complicated hairstyle. She saw her cheekbones and her fair skin, but her mother's dark eyes. There was not a day that she did not think about her mother. Lavinia missed her terribly.

"It is impolite to keep a gentleman waiting."

"Even if I haven't met the gentleman before tonight?" Lavinia asked with a smirk, as she dismissed the feelings of sadness that came with the memories of her mother.

"You know the answer to that question. I taught you well as your governess. Tonight is your opportunity to make me proud."

Lavinia patted her hair and turned to look at herself in the mirror one last time, "Charlotte, this rose dress. Is it a good colour for me? Should I change into the teal?"

"Oh no, you'll ruin your hair. If your maid has to set those curls again, she won't be happy. You look lovely – that rose is the perfect colour for you."

"Maybe I should wear the cream?"

"Come on now," Charlotte said as she grabbed Lavinia's hand. "With your money no-one will care what you're wearing."

Lavinia couldn't disagree. She followed Charlotte out of the room and together they raced along the hallway of the enormous country house owned by her grandmother. The corridor was lined with oil paintings of generations of Talridges – each one stared at Lavinia as she rushed past them. In the five years since she had first arrived at Claxton Hall, she had never ceased to be slightly worried that the paintings were haunted, with their great staring eyes always watching her.

As they rushed towards the great marble staircase, she remembered how she had been awed by the enormous rooms and high ceilings of the house, when she had come to live with her grandmother. The dark wood and damask, the upholstered furnishings – all were far more fantastic than she ever could have imagined, while growing up in Cotes Cross. Even nowadays, she was still awestruck by the wealth she saw on display around her.

"Stop! You do not want to look like you've been running," Charlotte whispered on the landing. "Your face is flushed. That will never do. Take a moment and breathe... Now, that's better. Maybe you'll just look like you have rosy cheeks. A woman who exerts herself is not going to attract a husband, remember that."

"What if I do not want a husband?"

"Shhh! If your grandmother hears that, she'll be wretched. You *do* want a husband, *every* woman does."

Lavinia nodded her head. "Very well, I can see that I will not win this argument. But have you not noticed that the gentlemen don't seem to take notice of me, much less set their hearts on me?"

"No, you silly girl," Charlotte giggled. "We'd best be quiet, or our guests may hear us on the stairs, laughing like children."

Inside, Lavinia still felt like a child, even though she was a young woman. Her character had always been that of a retiring, timid person who had moments of precociousness that were unexpected. She preferred her books and her embroidery to almost everything else; however, her grandmother insisted that she meet every eligible young gentleman in the county. After all that her grandmother had done for her, she could not refuse yet another introduction.

"Why should this gentleman be any different? Oh, Charlotte you go... you marry whoever it is in the drawing room." Lavinia whispered.

"I would, but I am a penniless companion, remember? I think you may want to meet this man, although you may know him already. He's the son of a viscount."

"The son of a viscount – here in the drawing room? Who is it?"

"You will soon see. Now be confident, you hear. You are going to be Miss Talridge."

"Miss Lavinia Dean Talridge."

"Be whoever you like, but we cannot waste another moment."

Lavinia did not know why her grandmother insisted that they go through all of this over and over. She had been formally introduced to nearly every eligible young man within a twenty-mile radius. Each time the result had been the same – polite conversation, a hand or two of cards, and she may even have played the pianoforte. Then there would be the goodbyes. Although she possessed a generous dowry, she was not the heiress to Claxton Hall. Mrs Talridge's nephew, an older man whose business in the East Indies kept him occupied, was set to inherit the estate, leaving Lavinia with her dowry and her annuity.

Lavinia sometimes wondered if she was not pursued by the young men who knew her family and her grandmother, because the unfortunate details of her birth were known. Were they the reason she was unwed, despite her grandmother's efforts?

"Smile, look beautiful, and remember everything I taught you," Charlotte reminded her at the door of the drawing room.

Lavinia stood up straight, smoothing the rose satin of her dress. She told herself that she was a good-looking woman with a modest fortune. She was worthy of being the wife of any man (except maybe for the Prince Regent himself). With her own silent dialogue of everything optimistic that her grandmother and Charlotte had ever told her, she smiled and entered the room, with Charlotte behind her.

The drawing room, in its magnificent gilded glory, was one of Lavinia's favourite rooms, except on nights when there were dinner guests. It was the epitome of refinement and opulence. The walls were white with gilt trim, and the sconces and the chandeliers were crystal and brass. Everything from the furniture to the rugs, was in shades of green, turquoise, and rose. She had to admit that her grandmother had excellent taste, keeping up with the latest trends of fashion in architecture and dress, and her furnishings especially reflected the classical taste of London and the gilt of the previous age.

Amongst the usual assortment of local dignitaries and notable citizens, was the addition of two men who Lavinia recognised from church and various social functions that summer. She had never been formally introduced to either man, but she knew them by reputation.

The Viscount of Wharton stood by the mantle of the fireplace. He looked as though he was avoiding mingling with anyone of a lesser rank. He was a tall, gaunt man with grey hair and a face that may have once been handsome, but now was firmly set in a scowl. Beside him was a younger gentleman who shared his height. He was not a corpulent man nor was he thin. He possessed the build of an avid outdoorsman; his waist was trim, and his shoulders were broad and strong. His wavy hair was lighter than Lavinia's, but that was not what struck her about him – it was his cold, unwavering facial expression, as if he was appraising her and everyone in the room.

"My dear, have you greeted Sir William Applegate and his wife? What of Mr and Mrs Newland?"

"No Grandmother, I have not greeted anyone. I have just arrived," Lavinia replied as her grandmother rushed to speak to her as soon as she entered the drawing room.

Mrs Talridge was undeterred. "It is just as well. Charlotte can do that for you. I have important guests I would like for you to meet."

Her grandmother steered her towards the two gentlemen who stood, alike in manner and aloofness, by the mantle. Mrs Talridge beamed with happiness as she made the formal introduction of her granddaughter to Lord Wharton and his younger son, Mr George Keeling. If Lavinia had presumed that she was being appraised when she entered the room, she felt even more so now that she stood directly in front of Mr Keeling.

His eyes were a shade of green that she assumed must have been striking when they were not narrowed. His chin was blunt, and his cheekbones were high. He possessed the kind of handsome countenance that she was accustomed to seeing in paintings. He stood a head taller than she, which she would not have minded in the least, except that he was staring down at her as if she was an annoyance.

"Lord Wharton, I do not feel that there would be the slightest impropriety if we allowed my granddaughter and your son to speak to each other alone, here in the drawing room. I was hoping to get your opinion concerning a business matter. I do look to your expert opinion on matters regarding my interests."

"As you wish, Mrs Talridge," the viscount said in a disinterested manner, abruptly leaving Lavinia and Mr Keeling standing awkwardly beside the fireplace.

Lavinia remembered Charlotte's instructions to be pleasant and to ask about predictably boring topics. This turned out to be more of a struggle than she had anticipated, as her mind was a maelstrom of memories concerning the viscount and his family. A large portion of the village of Cotes Cross belonged to the viscount, and he also owned farms and cottages on the outskirts of the hamlet. She recalled that even as a child, she had heard of the cruelty and greed of the viscount. He had a reputation for evicting widows and of not caring if tenants were too ill to pay their rent. He also did not take any interest in the village or the villagers. As lord of the manor of Cotes Cross, the viscount, by custom, should have been the leading benefactor of the church and the charities of the village. He was not a patron to Cotes Cross; that responsibility fell to other prominent citizens such as Mrs Talridge, at Lavinia's urging.

When Lavinia looked at the viscount, she saw the bane of the people who called Cotes Cross home. There was hope that his eldest son and heir, Mr Denton Keeling, would be a better man than his father. That outcome was yet to be determined, as the father was still very much alive. When Lavinia looked at his younger son, the man who she was supposed to consider as a possible husband, she saw the same cruel stare and arrogance as that of his father. She could not think of any pleasant remarks or questions, nor did she wish to ask him about Cotes Cross.

"What a strange look you have about you, Miss – what was your name again? I seem to have forgotten," Mr Keeling said in a bored, disaffected manner.

"I am Miss Lavinia Dean Talridge. Do I have a strange look? I did not realise that I possessed anything strange about me."

"It is the way you look at *me*. It is odd for a woman."

"Odd? Sir? I do not mean to speak out of turn to a gentleman of your rank, but what an impertinent thing to say to a woman whom you have just met."

"I have no time for pleasantries... and I certainly do not intend to waste either your or my time by attempting to make polite conversation, just because it is expected."

Lavinia glanced behind her. She was looking for Charlotte, or anyone who could be an ally. Was she imagining his rude speech and behaviour? Did he truly intend to act as if he did not care about how he spoke to her when there was no-one around to hear it? He may be the second son of a viscount, but he was certainly not a gentleman.

"If we are to dispense with the pleasantries of polite conversation, perhaps I may ask you about a subject that is dear to me."

"What does it matter? Say whatever you wish, it makes no difference to me."

"Cotes Cross, what is your opinion of it?"

"I have no opinion. It is of little consequence to me."

"That is what I presumed, yet your father's agents are the landlords for many of the tenants in that village."

"That is one of several properties that belong to my family. Why should one insignificant village matter to me? It and all my father's estate will be inherited by my eldest brother. What use can they be to me?"

"I can see that it does not matter, not the village nor anyone who lives there. Forgive me if I show concern for those people who call the village home. I sure do not need to remind you that we are responsible for those less fortunate than us, no matter our station."

"I see no reason why we should continue this pretence of civility. If you will excuse me," he bowed his head, and then walked away from her, leaving her standing alone at the fireplace.

Lavinia was shocked. She had never met a man so rude, so boorish, and so arrogant in her life! Lavinia knew immediately that if Mr Keeling was this rude and intolerable, she would *never* agree to marry him.

From her vantage point, she surveyed the drawing room. Nobody seemed to have noticed what had just happened. Her grandmother was smiling and conducting a one-sided conversation with the viscount while Charlotte was embroiled in a discussion with a small circle of guests. Mr Keeling had disappeared.

Chapter 4

Luncheon was not common in all upper-class homes in Yorkshire, but Mrs Talridge insisted on luncheon every day at half past noon. It was a custom that was quite popular in London and so she adopted it at her country house, as well as at her house in Mayfair. That afternoon, the midday meal was cold pheasant, fresh-water fish in aspic, and boiled potatoes. The meal was one of Lavinia's favourites, but she found that her appetite disappeared as soon as her grandmother shared the news of the invitation that had arrived as they were being served.

"The viscount has sent an invitation for us to dine at his home at Brigham Park, the day after tomorrow. Isn't that exciting? Lavinia you must be pleased," Mrs Talridge exclaimed.

Lavinia was still reeling from the events of the previous evening. Mr Keeling had treated her as though she were a common char-woman. Perhaps, she decided, he was not quite that rude, but that was how he had made her feel. He had barely spoken to her and when he did have something to say, he hadn't even tried to conceal his contempt for her or anyone who was lower in rank than himself. She had to admit that she had been assertive when it came to Cotes Cross, but she felt strongly about the people who loved her.

In her memory, they were her people, her family for the first thirteen years of her life.

"Lavinia, do you not like the pheasant? You are just picking at your food," asked Charlotte. "Is it your nerves? Are you not thrilled to be seeing Mr Keeling again?"

"No, it is not nerves. I never want to see him again," Lavinia answered as she dropped her fork and knife onto the plate with a loud clattering sound.

"Lavinia, you know better than to make so much noise at luncheon. You are not a child!" her grandmother scolded.

"Sorry, grandmother, I was not thinking," Lavinia said as she picked her fork and knife up and then carefully placed them beside the plate. "Why has he invited us to dine at his house? When he was here, he looked as if he was stuck in a barnyard, and we were all pigs and goats. I have never seen a man look as filled with intolerable conceit as he was, with the exception of his son, Mr Keeling."

Charlotte gasped, "Lavinia! How can you say such awful things about your future father-in-law?"

"Charlotte, I did not yet have an occasion to tell you what Mr Keeling said to me last night," Lavinia replied as she looked at the footmen who were waiting to serve the following course and to keep the drinks poured.

"Perhaps you should wait until our afternoon walk in the garden," Charlotte said as she whispered the words. "Servants like to gossip."

Mrs Talridge looked perplexed. "What has come over you, my child? You are a sweet, composed girl... and now quite suddenly you are speaking ill about a gentleman who may very well be the father of your husband-to-be. Do I need to remind you that Charlotte is correct? The viscount is your superior in all manner of rank and property.

He is also your elder."

Lavinia frowned, "I know he is, but I find him unpleasant. I find his son to be arrogant and rude."

Mrs Talridge shook her head. "I hope you did not make the mistake of telling him he was arrogant and rude. How silly of me, of course you did not, how could you? The viscount would never have sent us an invitation to dine if his son knew that you find him to be a bore."

"He was *rude*. He said that attempting to make pleasant conversation with me was a waste of time!" answered Lavinia.

"Maybe he was nervous." suggested Charlotte as she sliced the pheasant into neat pieces on the gilt-trimmed china plate. "He may not have meant to say those things that caused you such distress. What if he did not intend to be rude? Men can behave differently to women and they are not always genteel in social situations."

"I know he meant the things he said – you should have seen how he looked at me. He looked at me as if I was something distasteful that he had found underneath his boot!" Lavinia exclaimed.

Mrs Talridge nearly choked on her food, as she laughed, "Lavinia, do not be so theatrical. Mr Keeling is a gentleman. As the son of a viscount, he would never behave rudely towards a lady and never look at her as you have described. I think you have misjudged him."

"I have not misjudged anything... not at all," answered Lavinia.

"You must have misunderstood him, my dear, after all, we have been invited to dine at their house. We shall see how you fare on that evening. Charlotte may be correct. Men who enjoy hunting and other sporting pursuits do not always perform at their best in a drawing room amongst strangers. We shall give him another chance when he is amongst his own family in familiar surroundings – yes, that is what we shall do," explained Lavinia's grandmother.

"A second chance to be rude to me and to treat me abominably? Must I go? Can you and Charlotte not dine without me?"

"Lavinia, you are showing your inexperience in the ways of the world. How can we go without you? You are the sole reason for the invitation. The viscount was pleased with you as a match for his son. Are you not as satisfied as I am by this happy news?" When Lavinia looked down, she continued more softly. "He confided in me last evening at dinner. He complimented your appearance, your fine playing at the piano, and your disposition. Take solace in the report I have given you," Mrs Talridge said with a smile, her exasperation forgotten.

Astonished, Lavinia dropped her napkin on her plate as she pushed away from the table. "If I intended to marry the viscount, I would be gladdened by his opinion of me. Yet, it is not his good opinion that I seek. I cannot find such flattering words about his son nor about him. How can I, when I know how I was treated... and how they have ignored the plight of the villagers of Cotes Cross?"

Charlotte looked concerned. "Lavinia, do I have to remind you of your manners? A lady never permits her emotions to get the better of her."

Lavinia was not in the mood to be lectured. "I am not a lady. I am the daughter of a seamstress from Cotes Cross."

Her grandmother spoke sternly, but in a calm tone, as she answered her granddaughter, "You are not that girl, not anymore. There is no need for this outburst. It is inconsiderate to spoil the appetites of Charlotte and myself because you cannot control your temper. Sit down at once and remain silent if you have nothing better to say."

Lavinia knew her grandmother was overjoyed with the invitation. Even more than the invitation, her grandmother was thrilled that Lavinia may become a Keeling. Lavinia sat down as she did not wish to disappoint her grandmother or Charlotte. Frowning, she took a deep breath, "I do not know what came over me. I have never been so angry, but when I think of Mr Keeling, I am furious. Maybe I am being too theatrical, but I just see him in a different light I suppose."

"Could you be mistaken about Mr Keeling and his authority over Cotes Cross? I have *never* heard anything detrimental said about him, not in my presence," her grandmother said reassuringly as she resumed eating her lunch.

"I do not think so, but I only met him once... he did say that his brother, Denton, was the heir to Cotes Cross and all of their father's property."

"What if he does care about the village, but it is not his duty?" Lavinia's grandmother exclaimed.

Lavinia looked at Charlotte and her grandmother, "Have I been so blinded by his conceit that I assumed he was villainous?"

"That's better. That's the level-headed, practical Lavinia I know. Why don't we go to dinner and judge, then, if he improves upon the second meeting. If he is still as boorish as you have presumed, then you have confirmed that you were right – but if, on the other hand, he proves to be charming, then you may admit that you have been happily in error. What a joyous blunder to discover that on a second look, things are not as bad as they first appeared. What do you say? Shall you join me in my satisfaction that we have secured an invitation to

Brigham Park?"

Deep inside Lavinia doubted that Mr Keeling would act in any way differently to how he had behaved at Claxton Hall. She was willing to give him a second chance, but she did not expect that he would be able to alter her opinion of him, at least not significantly.

As the luncheon came to an end, she listened as her grandmother cheerfully expounded on her plans for the match and how splendid it would be for Lavinia. After the footmen had cleared away the last of the courses, Lavinia sought the sanctuary of the garden and Mrs Talridge retired to the study to answer correspondence and to oversee the estate's accounts.

In the walled garden of Claxton Hall, Lavinia, who was joined by Charlotte, was finally at liberty to speak with candour as they strolled along the paths beside the pond.

Charlotte began the conversation with a warning. "Lavinia, I do not wish to lecture you. I may no longer be your governess, but as I am your friend, I should warn you that whatever you choose to say in the presence of a footman or maid may find its way out of this house. You must have a care in such matters, especially concerning an influential man such as the viscount."

"I feel terrible for allowing my emotions to rule my good sense, but if you had only heard what Mr Keeling said to me. If you had seen how he looked at me, with your own eyes, you would understand why I am so vexed with him."

"Vexed or not, you must maintain your control at all times. You nearly sent your grandmother into a fit. She was so happy to tell you about the invitation. Did you see your grandmother's face? Poor woman, I thought we would have to summon aid. Oh, I shouldn't have said that. That was a terrible thing to say about my employer. She has been so generous, paying me to be your companion when she might have discharged me," Charlotte paused for a second and then quickly turned back to Lavinia. "You nearly stormed out of luncheon, as if you had no breeding or decorum of any kind."

"I am sorry for that... I did not intend to behave so rashly. Do not make me feel any worse than I already do. I should have moderated my anger. I know well that my grandmother could have left me in Cotes Cross or insisted that I be sent off to school. Instead, she has permitted me to live in this fine house and given me a life of ease." Lavinia looked into Charlotte's eyes. "You have reminded me of my own failings in showing my gratitude for my grandmother's generosity, and I give you my word that I will not allow my emotions to have their command of me ever again."

"We shall speak no more about it," said Charlotte with a tender voice. "You are still young, and I will try to remember that. When it comes to matters of the heart, emotions can run wild if we are not diligent. Since we have no-one to overhear our conversation, you may tell me what happened last night, if you wish."

"I wanted to tell you last night, but the hour was so late, and our guests tarried in leaving. I began to despair that they would not leave before dawn's first light. It was terrible, but I suppose I must admit that I may be to blame for the outcome," Lavinia said.

"How are you to blame? I have taught you how to act and what to say in all manner of society. You are being honoured with an invitation to Brigham Park, so you must have behaved beautifully. Perhaps you are overwrought?"

"I am not overwrought... at least, I do not think so. I am ashamed that I was so brash, but that is the effect that Mr Keeling has upon me, I am embarrassed to say."

"We shall both endeavour to be far more respectful of your dear grandmother," said Charlotte calmly, "but shall we return to the subject that we were not at liberty to discuss at luncheon – Mr Keeling? How very interesting that a gentleman could have such a marked effect on your disposition in such a short amount of time?" she mused.

Lavinia could barely contain her ire as she replied, "A marked effect? Is that what you choose to call the dissatisfaction and vexation that I feel? He is the sole cause of my outburst; his behaviour was far below what I would expect of a man in his station. When I compare his lack of manners to the men of Cotes Cross, I find that Mr Keeling has less gentility than a common field hand!"

Charlotte gasped in surprise. Startled, she quickly looked around the garden, "Oh! Lavinia! I do hope no-one else has heard you say such things. The son of a viscount compared to a commoner? What has happened to you? I have never known you to say such things!"

"It is true. When I was the poor daughter of a seamstress, I was shown more respect by men who laboured, than I was shown by a man of education and class."

"Lavinia, did you not hear a word I said at luncheon? He may have been suffering from reserve or perhaps that is his manner? The nobility are not the same as you and I. Your perception of his coarseness may have been a result of your own inexperience with men of his rank."

"If *that* is how the upper classes act, then I shall be happy to seek a husband amongst the ranks of common men."

"Lavinia Talridge! You must not say such a thing, or if you do please make certain that your grandmother shall never hear of it! She is in good health for her age, but I do wonder if such a sentiment, expressed by you, wouldn't send her straight to her bed chamber with despair!"

"Despair? What of my own despair? He did not care one whit for Cotes Cross. I asked him, and he said so! He called my home insignificant. He did not attempt to conceal his lack of care about the people I knew."

"Lavinia, that village is no longer your home. You are no longer that girl anymore. Besides, what do you expect of him? Did you allow yourself the indulgence of believing that a gentleman of his wealth and breeding would be concerned about a small hamlet that comprises part of his father's vast estate? If you asked him to name all of the members of his father's domestic staff, could he do so, and would you hold him accountable if he could not? For that matter, do you know the names of the kitchen staff here at Claxton Hall?"

Lavinia stopped walking and stared at Charlotte, her eyes fixed on her companion's bright visage. She thought of Charlotte's question. She was perplexed by the answer and was forced to admit, "I may not know every kitchen maid's name, but I would care if some calamity should befall them."

"Providing you knew of the calamity. Do be reasonable, I do not know why you have decided that he should be judged so harshly. Consider your position on the matter and think about it practically. The plight of your former village may seem of little consequence to a gentleman who barely considers its existence."

"He *should* consider it. He *should* care."

"Perhaps you mean that his family should care for their tenants in the manner of all good landlords? Honestly Lavinia, he is a young man, not much older than yourself. It is doubtful that he will inherit his father's title or estate. Mr Keeling is forced to seek his fortune outside of his home. Why should a village or any other part of his father's holdings interest him?"

"How peculiar, Charlotte, he said much the same thing to me last night. At the time I mistook it for arrogance, but now I see that maybe I did misjudge him concerning the matter."

"Perhaps you would be wise to re-examine your position regarding Mr Keeling."

Lavinia held up her head as though she was wounded by the idea that she was mistaken. "I will re-examine my position, but it will do little to alter my opinion about his behaviour towards me. Rude or not, his haughtiness and inconsiderate tone will not leave my memory, simply because I wish it. He shall have to go very far indeed to alter my opinion of him."

Charlotte slid her arm into Lavinia's, as she urged her to return to their walk. "He may go very far – you shall have the pleasure of discovering that at the dinner. Tell me Lavinia, when you are not vexed by the gentleman, can you not concede that he *is* handsome?"

Lavinia thought for a second and then smiled cheekily. "Humph! He may be handsome, but I will not allow my head to be turned by his countenance alone. I would rather marry an ill-favoured pig farmer than a handsome lord!"

"Lavinia!" giggled Charlotte. "Have you forgotten all of my counsel?"

"Not at all, but I will not marry a man such as Mr Keeling – not if he insists on treating me like a maid!"

"Maid or not, if you become his wife, it won't matter how he treats you. You will become the daughter-in-law of a viscount! Would that not be worth any ill temper or poor manners?"

"Perhaps for you, dear Charlotte... but I want... more. I want to discover for myself if I *may* be loved or that I may *not* want to marry at all... Is there not time to learn what *I* want?"

"No, my dear, there is not. Your grandmother will not rest until your future is assured and settled. From what she has said about the viscount, he *is* of a similar opinion regarding his son."

"Oh Charlotte, if only I was in Cotes Cross again with only the rent and food as my concerns – I should think myself much happier."

"You might be happier, but you would not be so well dressed or well fed. No more talk of Cotes Cross or anything else frivolous. We have something else urgent to discuss."

Lavinia felt a moment of anxiety as she asked, "What is it? What is urgent?"

"I do not mean to cause you any alarm, but we have a matter to discuss which may decide your future. A crucial one. What are you going to wear to Brigham Park?"

Lavinia wanted to laugh at the stern tone of her companion's question. Her choice of a dress for the dinner was not nearly as important to her as it was to Charlotte. Lavinia concealed her urge to dismiss Charlotte's concerns and listened to her catalogue her wardrobe, all the while thinking about Mr Keeling and her future. If he suddenly treated her as a gentleman should treat a lady, would she desire him for a husband? Would she desire any man for that position?

These were questions that she knew would be answered all too quickly and that caused her to silently despair.

Chapter 5

Brigham Park was a vast estate set on the moors of Yorkshire. The dark-grey stone of the medieval ramparts and turrets gave the house an imposing air that made Lavinia wonder if she and her companions had magically travelled back in time. With its high, slender windows, gothic peaks, and balustrades, the house seemed less a residence and more like an ancient fortified castle. Siting high upon a hillside, it loomed giant, dark, and intimidating.

In the warm, golden light of the setting sun, she watched as a brigade of servants lit torches along the roadway, moving swiftly amongst the rocks and low brush. As the carriage made its way across a stone bridge, she peered out of the window, while her companions remained seated against the velvet-cushioned upholstery. Neither lady appeared to take any notice of the house, conveying a disinterest in the majestic surroundings.

"Lavinia do sit back in your seat. Do you want any of the servants to whisper to their master that you behaved as though you were without manners?" admonished Mrs Talridge.

"I want to see if there's a moat. In all the stories I have read, castles always have moats," Lavinia answered.

"There is no moat, not anymore," her grandmother answered.

"You surprise me Lavinia, I did not think you cared to see Brigham Park," teased Charlotte.

"It is not that I did not care to see the house. I have misgivings concerning the gentleman who owns it," Lavinia replied, but she did as her grandmother ordered and sat back from the window.

With a clucking sound, her grandmother signalled her disgust, "I will have no more of that talk, not this evening."

"I am sorry grandmother. I will do my best not to cause any embarrassment to you or Charlotte. Why did you not tell me that the viscount lived in a castle? It would have spared me the surprise," Lavinia answered as she held a gloved hand to her hair. "I do hope my hair stays pinned, as I am not accustomed to this style."

Mrs Talridge laughed, "You are so young my dear. Worried about your hair in one moment and this great house in the next. I am not as astounded as you by this residence, because I have visited this house on rare occasions over the course of my years at Claxton Hall. I admit that Brigham Park is quite impressive, but I should not wish to have it as my own, at my advanced age. The rooms have a chill to them that never dissipates, even in the summer months. I find the draughtiness and the cold to be a danger to my health. I do not know how the viscount takes his ease in such a place, but I doubt that a man of his son's age would notice such things."

Lavinia wondered if she would find the rooms to be cold. The only thing she suspected would bring a chill would be the presence of Mr Keeling. Dismissing her judgment, she recalled the promise she had made, both to her grandmother and to Charlotte, that she would not be so quick to form an opinion of Mr Keeling. At least, they had reminded her, not until she had spoken to him here at his home. They were convinced that at his house, she would see him as he was – the son of an important and rich nobleman.

As the team of four horses drew the carriage into the walled court-yard of Brigham Park, Lavinia was convinced that her heart was beat-ing as loudly as the sound the horses' hooves made against the stone. As the carriage came to a stop, she wondered if anyone else from her old village had ever dined there as an honoured dinner guest. Her anx-iety made her question why she had ever agreed to attend the dinner, but this thought was interrupted when her grandmother reached out to her.

Putting her hand on Lavinia's knee, her grandmother smiled at her as she said, "Lavinia, you look lovely. Do not forget to act as you look, and you will always do well. Come, we mustn't be late, after all, you are the guest of honour on this night."

"I cannot be the guest of honour, not here," Lavinia replied as the footman held the carriage door open.

Charlotte answered, "You may not truly be the guest of honour, but you are the reason we have been invited here this evening. Please do not forget that. This may well be a night to remember – the first night you are to dine at the home of the gentleman who may become your husband."

Lavinia nodded her head, careful not to move too much lest she upset the curls and ribbons running through her hair. As they stepped down from the carriage, a stiff breeze blew through the courtyard, wailing softly, and mournful in its cries. Torches blazed from the ram-parts and candlelight glowed from the windows, as she looked at the house.

"Stop gawking! You are a lady, remember." Charlotte whispered to Lavinia.

Silently Lavinia looked down at her dress, smoothing the material of its wrinkles. In the light of the torches, the silvery netting and bead-work glittered against the periwinkle fabric of the gown. Her grand-mother had told her that the colour was very becoming, and Lavinia was disposed to believe her, hoping that the gown was fashionable enough for a dinner at such a grand residence.

After entering through the great oaken door, the ladies of the party were received by the viscount and both his sons, Mr Denton Keeling and Mr George Keeling. Lavinia did not see a viscountess, nor did she meet any other members of their family. For the briefest of minutes, she speculated whether the family was comprised of so few members, but her thoughts were soon lost to the awe she felt in her surround-ings. The entrance to the house was as imposing as the exterior. Walk-ing into the hall, she maintained her composure although she felt in-significant compared to the coat of arms carved over the enormous stone fireplace. The dark stone walls were covered in tapestries that surely must have been as ancient as the house. Under her slippered feet were pavers as cold and grey as the stone of the walls, and amongst the tapestries were coats of arms, swords, long wickedly-bladed weapons, and pikes displayed in a dramatic fashion as though this keep, this house, may at some time in the future return to its war-like origins.

Past the vast hall, Lavinia followed behind the party, as they were shown into the drawing room. The drawing room was less intimidat-ing than the hall, but no less impressive. A fireplace that could have accommodated their entire group within its confines, burned with a fire from logs as long and nearly as wide as Lavinia. Oil paintings hung on the dark wood-panelled walls. The furniture was a deep crimson colour, and embroidered in Elizabethan and Jacobean patterns, as were the rugs underfoot. As she examined the room in detail, Lavinia seemed to feel as though she had truly fallen into a fairy realm, where time had reverted to the distant past.

She was jarred out of her reverie by the voice of Mr Denton Keeling, the heir to the title and the estate.

"Miss Talridge, how delightful that you have joined us for dinner," he said in a manner that was brusque but polite.

He resembled his father and younger brother in the shade of his hair and build. His features were similar, but that was where the resemblance ended. Although enormously wealthy and well attired, he was the model of decorum. His speech and manner were as Charlotte had suggested, indicative of his rank and status. Although he was not overly expressive of any emotions or sentiment, Lavinia found his cool detachment to be not displeasing. He spoke correctly, addressing her with civility, but there was something in his look, in the manner of his conversing, that put her at ease.

With a curtsy, she nodded her head before answering, "I was pleased to receive the invitation. Is the dinner party to be a large one?"

"Not this evening. My father thinks, and I share his opinion, that in matters such as this, a smaller party would be more in order. Don't you agree?"

Lavinia did not know if she agreed or not. She wished that there would be a larger group to dine – perhaps she may find someone she knew well, who would act as a distraction. She wished for someone who might ease her anxiousness in a way that Charlotte and her grandmother could not. She wished for an ally, but quickly became resigned to the fact that there would most likely be no companions who understood her unease, that evening.

She looked at the face of the next Viscount of Wharton, and responded, "Yes I agree. Small parties can be charming in their way."

"They can be charming, and I hope you find everything at Brigham Park to be to your liking," Mr Denton Keeling replied as they were joined by his younger brother. "It appears that my brother wishes to address you. I shall receive your grandmother and her companion. They appear to be in need of a man of my charm and wit."

He bowed gracefully as he departed. Once again, Lavinia was left alone with the man she thought she abhorred. As there was no-one else in the drawing room, she wondered if that was the sole reason why Mr Keeling had ventured to his brother's side. Looking up at him, she noticed that he did not appear to be as stern as he had seemed during his recent visit to Claxton Hall.

"Miss Talridge, I see that my brother had done an admirable job of welcoming you to Brigham Park."

"He has done all that was required of a gracious host," Lavinia answered, uncertain what to make of the elder brother or of Mr Keeling's politeness.

"I trust you are well, as are your grandmother and Miss Fenwick?" he asked as he nodded in the direction of her party.

"They are well, thank you. And how are you and your father? I see your father is in good health," she asked, as she followed Charlotte's instructions regarding polite conversation. How many times had Lavinia heard Charlotte's suggestion to always inquire about health, the weather, and other similar subjects. Tonight, she was heeding that advice.

"We are all well and in perfect health, thank you. How was the carriage ride – I hope you did not find the journey too taxing?"

"Not at all. I rather enjoyed the views of the moors from the roadway. The beauty of the moors during the summer months, is always a source of pleasure for me. The transformation is remarkable, from grey and bleak to green and growing," she answered as she became aware that she may be speaking too much about herself. Recalling Charlotte's other instructions to ask questions of a gentleman, to ensure that he was the subject of the conversation, she immediately asked, "Have you had an opportunity to do much riding this season?"

As Mr Keeling answered her question, she looked at him, studying his face and features. He was no less abrupt in his manner, nor was he any warmer in the delivery of his chosen words, but he seemed different this evening. While he lacked his brother's obvious charm, Lavinia felt that the gentleman standing in front of her, appeared to be the man she had met before, but his former disdain for her seemed to have vanished.

"That is why I prefer a steed of Spanish stock over the Irish breeds," he said, as Lavinia sensed a pause in the conversation.

Smiling and nodding to indicate that she had been paying attention, although she had not been for the better part of five minutes, she tried to think of a suitable question that would reflect her attention to his interests but could not find one. Riding and equestrian pursuits were not activities she found to be enjoyable. Horses had always made her nervous and riding was not something that came easily to her. With a glance through the doorway of the drawing room, she caught a glimpse of a suit of armour, and with renewed inspiration, she decided to change tactics.

"I find the relics displayed in the hall to be fascinating. Did your ancestors wear them into battle?" Lavinia was inwardly cringing at the naivety of her question but managed to smile at Mr Keeling instead. Perhaps he wouldn't consider her ignorant for asking such a ridiculously obvious query.

Smiling, he shook his head. "What an inquisitive mind you possess, Miss Talridge."

She was struck by his smile. This was the first time she had ever seen it. He could be a handsome man, if only he was as warm and polite as his brother. With a slightly disinterested air, he said, "Would you like me to tell you the history of the house?"

"Yes, I find myself curious about the age of this residence," she answered.

"Very well... the house itself was once a fortress, built by the first Viscount of Wharton. That was several centuries ago when the border between Scotland and England was in a state of constant war. We are many miles from the present-day border, but that did not save Yorkshire. Armies would come down from the north; bands of marauders and soldiers would sweep in through the countryside causing trouble, burning fields, crops, and villages. It was a lawless time. Fortresses such as this keep were constructed. By the end of the disputes, the keep had grown to include this residence, the towers you see high above the courtyard, and the newly added conservatory."

Lavinia listened as he spoke about the house's history. He spoke with the detachment of one who had repeated these same words many times before, and while Lavinia paid attention to the history, she could not conjure the same feelings for the man who was speaking, as she could manufacture interest in the subject of Brigham Park. As much as she wished otherwise, even with his marked change in temperament, he still seemed as distant and cold as the paintings hanging from the walls.

"Do you have any other questions regarding the history of the house?" he asked as he looked slightly past her.

It was then that she realised that he was not addressing her in any meaningful way. He did not look at her face when he spoke and did not even seem genuinely interested in the history of his own home.

Looking over her shoulder at the small party behind her, which was comprised of Mr Denton Keeling, Charlotte Fenwick, her grandmother, and the viscount, she would have preferred to be in their company. Sighing, she tried to think of anything to ask that wouldn't strike her host as sounding common or uneducated, but she was at a loss as to what to say. Waiting for Mr Keeling to speak was nearly as agonizing as avoiding questions about the things she really wished to know the answers to, such as what the cause of his new-found politeness was.

"Miss Talridge, would you care to accompany me to the dining room?" Mr Keeling asked as he held out his arm to her.

She glanced at him, hesitant for a moment, as though she was misreading his actions. By the rules of precedence, her grandmother should be accompanied by the viscount. Mr Denton Keeling should accompany her, and Charlotte, the lowest ranked woman, would be accompanied by Mr George Keeling, unless she was engaged or wed to him, which would make his accompaniment excusable. Unsure of what to make of his actions, she stared at his proffered arm, as though if she accepted, then she would be committing herself to marriage.

"Miss Talridge, the others are waiting. We mustn't delay," he said coolly.

Feeling her cheeks turn crimson with embarrassment and confusion, she placed her gloved hand on his arm, accepting his gesture of politeness. He escorted her into the dining room, a room as lavishly decorated as the drawing room. A table, that could seat fifty or more, stood in the centre of the room under a high vaulted ceiling. Tall gothic windows and medieval iron chandeliers reminded her of the room's historic past. Shivering, despite the heat of the roaring fire and the season, she allowed herself to be seated beside Mr Keeling at the table, and across from Charlotte.

Being that near to him, she should have felt gladness that he was handsome, and she should have noticed a softening of her opinion towards him, but there was none. He rarely glanced in her direction and when he did, she felt that he was not truly looking at her. Her original observation that he was looking past her, seemed to hold true as much in the dining room as in the drawing room. She was struck by his behaviour – polite and yet as indistinguishable from the stone of the walls. He seemed to be like the footmen surrounding them – a man who was duty-bound by honour and decorum, and incapable of treating her with even feigned charm.

After examining her own reaction to him, she realised that she was far more anxious about saying the wrong things or her behaviour reflecting badly on her grandmother, than she was about garnering the good opinion of Mr Keeling. In all the great poetry of old that expounded on the high ideal of love, there was never a mention of the dullness of emotion she felt in his presence. With his imposing features and captivating green eyes, he could have stolen the heart of any woman, she surmised, except for her own. To her dismay, she found that she no longer loathed him, but he had done nothing to gain her favour. Suppressing the urge to shiver, she found that her opinion of Mr Keeling had remained steady throughout the course of the evening. Never wavering, like the cold that seeped in through the stone walls, he lacked warmth or interest, aside from the history of his surroundings and his family.

If her own judgement of Mr Keeling had altered from "detestable aristocrat" to "dutiful but uninteresting son of a viscount", she was not surprised that her grandmother's estimation had remained steadfast. To her dismay, she also suspected that Charlotte also remained as cheerful about the match as Mrs Talridge. Both ladies did not hesitate to glance towards Lavinia, smiling and offering silent expressions that could only be described as encouraging. How Lavinia wished she might draw them aside in private consultation to explain the deep and vast feeling of disenchantment she felt in the presence of Mr Keeling. Would they understand that he appeared, at second examination, to be unlike any man she would wish to marry, except in his appearance? He was exceptionally handsome, of that she could not be dissuaded, but his dullness, his very air of disinterest and dissatisfaction, did much to erode her view of his pleasant visage.

It was not surprising to her in the least that her own small party were not the only people who seemed to be observing her and Mr Keeling surreptitiously. It may have been her fanciful imagination, but she thought she noticed the viscount himself sternly watching his son and, on more than one occasion, she felt the weight of the elder son's stares.

The contented sound of Charlotte's voice carried across the dinner table and later to the drawing room. The fact that she was obviously enjoying the company of Mr Denton Keeling, was distasteful to Lavinia, not because of any jealousy arising from emotions regarding Mr Keeling's eldest brother, but because the heir to Brigham Park seemed to be a far more outgoing and charismatic dinner companion. How she wished Mr Keeling could be more like his eldest brother in charm and deportment!

When the evening came to a close, the only regret that Lavinia expressed, was not being given a tour of the grounds, which she found to be beautiful and fascinating. She did not have any wish, other than one of academic interest, to return to Brigham Park, although she soon learned that she was quite alone in her opinion. From the moment she settled into the seat of the carriage and the door was closed by the footman, her grandmother expressed her rapturous joy at the outcome of the evening.

"Lavinia, my dear, how radiant you appeared! How well you presented yourself. I have never been prouder of you than I am at this very moment! Indeed, is there a word that conveys a stronger sentiment? If there were such a word, I should speak it at once, do you hear me, child? How I have longed for this moment, for you... and how hard *you* have worked under Charlotte's tutelage to be the kind of lady that a gentleman such as Mr Keeling would fancy for a wife!"

Lavinia thought that nothing she could have shared would dampen her grandmother's spirits, however the truth, as Lavinia saw it, was quite different. She longed to offer her opinion, but was not as quick as Charlotte, to speak next.

"How dashing Mr Denton Keeling is, even though he is not as handsome as his brother. Was I alone in my observation that you and Mr Keeling were able to converse this evening? It appeared that he hardly left your company for even a moment!" Charlotte gushed, as she gently nudged Lavinia.

It now appeared that there were two sets of erroneous opinions that must be dashed to pieces with the truth. Lavinia sighed, taking a moment to gather her wits. She felt the air of expectation upon her as she slowly gave her companions an ounce of truth in their happy follies.

"My dear grandmother, and dear Charlotte, your confidence does my heart good... but I fear that I must be the voice of truth. I know that you do not wish to hear what I have to say to you. I have no wish to disturb your happiness... but... I must tell you that as altered as I found Mr Keeling to be, he was not so altered that I imagine he will express any desire to become my husband. I found him to be cold and disinterested. He was polite, but he was not affected by either my words or my presence," Lavinia revealed, feeling a deep satisfaction that she had spoken the truth.

For a moment, there was silence.

"You found Mr Keeling to be cold and disinterested?" Mrs Talridge replied. "My dear, that is the custom of the genteel classes. They do not convey their emotions in the same manner as do the commoners below them. Perhaps I have done a great disservice by not insisting that we associate with more titled gentry than we have since you became of marriageable age."

"Lavinia," Charlotte began, her voice steady and even, "If I may offer you my counsel on this matter. Please do not make the mistake of taking Mr Keeling's apparent insufficiency of warmth, as a sign of his lack of interest. In my experience of gentlemen of his position, they seldom disclose their feelings and rarely appear to be compelled by their emotions in any fashion. If he was speaking to you and did not attempt to resist your efforts at conversation, then he may be inclined to hold you in higher regard than you realise."

"See? There you are!" Mrs Talridge replied quickly, her spirits undamped. "You have it on both my and Charlotte's authority that Mr Keeling is not as disinterested as he may at first have appeared." Without giving Lavinia time to respond, she continued with a voice filled with anticipation. "I have something else to tell you... something that I think you will find exciting!"

Lavinia did not think that either Charlotte or her grandmother had truly listened to her concerns about Mr Keeling. She presumed and was becoming more convinced of it with every passing minute, that nothing she could say *would* change her grandmother's certainty, nor Charlotte's exuberance.

"What turn of events will I find exciting?" asked Lavinia.

Mrs Talridge's enthusiasm could hardly be contained as she said, "Why the viscount has grown even more convinced that you would make a perfect companion for his son. You may not be as aware that he observed you this evening, as I was. He confided in me that his good opinion, formed at Claxton Hall, has been confirmed by your behaviour this very evening. Do you understand what I am trying to tell you? The viscount is as much impressed by you as he was at your introduction. If *he* is impressed, then *you* can soon count yourself married to his son, I would wager!"

Her grandmother's words echoed in her thoughts, and the journey back to Claxton Hall was filled with chatter and the making of plans for the wedding. Lavinia wanted to remind her grandmother and Charlotte that Mr Keeling had not proposed to her, nor had he expressed any interest in doing so. It seemed really silly that his actions could be swayed, simply because his father had chosen her as his son's bride. If only she could find the right words to say to her companions, to cease their joyous prattle, but she could think of nothing that would deter them.

Sitting back in the carriage seat, she feigned fatigue, and as she closed her eyes, the sounds of their voices, like the chattering of birds, lulled her into a somnolent world of dreams.

Chapter 6

Lavinia had been convinced that Mr Keeling had not showed the slightest bit of interest in entering into the bond of marriage with her, but she was soon confronted by troubling evidence to the contrary. In the week following the dinner party at Brigham Park, he invited her to join him for tea, in the company of his brother and Charlotte Fenwick of course. That was soon followed by an invitation from Claxton Hall for tea, and then another for a weekend of shooting and sporting. Inevitably these social engagements included a dinner and ball to be held at Brigham Park.

The whirl of events had convinced Lavinia that her grandmother and Charlotte were correct in their assumptions. The viscount appeared to be plotting... perhaps that was too harsh a word, Lavinia thought... he was planning to see his son wed to her by the Christmas season. That was the most recent news that Charlotte had shared with her as they dismissed the maid and set about unpacking their traveling trunks at Brigham Park.

Charlotte smoothed a lilac dress festooned with cream coloured silk ribbon and flowers as she said, "Lavinia, isn't it exciting to be invited to a ball, here at Brigham Park? I do not know who is more excited by the prospect, your grandmother or I? I shall hate to see you wed, as I shall have to seek another position, but as your friend, I shall be satisfied that your future is secure."

Lavinia dropped the dress she was holding onto the curtained four-poster bed as she answered, "If only it was your wedding we were discussing. Do you not think it is strange that all of these rumours are circulating about my marriage, to the point of suggesting when I will be wed, yet the man who is to become my husband has not made a single mention of any such plans?"

"Why, of course he hasn't said anything to you... do not be foolish! A man of his position will not speak about marriage until all the details of the dowry and your annuity are settled. I am sure there will be no trouble regarding your wealth. Your grandmother is not just accepting, she is positively jovial, concerning your upcoming marriage. I cannot recall ever seeing her so delighted!"

"*She* is delighted? What about *me*? *Or* Mr Keeling for that matter? *He* never looks delighted. He has never tried to hold my hand or steal a kiss. He hardly looks at me and when he does, I sense that he is appraising me as he did upon our introduction. I feel like I am a horse or a piece of furniture that he is examining, in order to consider whether or not he should purchase it."

"Lavinia! How you speak sometimes! Comparing yourself to a horse is scandalous! I hope you do not intend to share your views with him before he marries you. If you did, he may reconsider his decision to make you his wife!"

"Reconsider, Charlotte? I wish someone would tell me when he ever considered it? He has yet to indicate even the slightest affection for me. Is that not strange?"

"Not in the least! Amongst the upper class, it is considered terrible form to display one's emotions. What do you wish him to do? Follow you about like a common shepherd or odd-job man, making impassioned speeches to you to assure you of his regard? He is the son of a viscount. If he shows you the slightest attention at all, you may rely on it that he is considering you for a bride."

Lavinia slumped across the bed. "If he is this romantic now, how will he be after we're married? It is astonishing that his line did not die out generations ago, if this is how the upper class Keelings entice their mates."

"Mates? You mustn't say such things, you sound like a commoner."

"I am a commoner."

"Not since I taught you differently. You cannot use that as an excuse for bad behaviour. If I tell you something, do you promise you will not be vexed with me?" Charlotte asked as she leaned against the bed post.

"Charlotte, aside from your overly optimistic view of Mr Keeling's regard for me, I cannot find any circumstance under which I should be truly vexed with you."

"If you give me your word..."

"You have my word, dear Charlotte. Now, tell me what you have to say that you are worried will vex me?"

"Lavinia, my friend, I have watched you and Mr Keeling together these past weeks. I do wonder if the reason why he has not proposed to you, or expressed any interest at all," Charlotte said, hesitating as she spoke, "is because of *you*?"

"*Me*? You think that he hasn't proposed to me because of something I may have done? Well..." she thought for a while. "That makes sense I suppose. I am not sure what you mean by that, but I am not vexed in the slightest."

"Do you not understand? You accuse him of being distant, but it is *you* who have been cold in your disposition. You offer him no encouragement or any indication that you have feelings that may lean towards matrimony."

"I have not offered him any encouragement because I do not wish to be married to him."

"What? You do not wish to become his wife?"

"No, I do not. From his actions towards me, I think he is of the same mind."

"Lavinia, this is dreadful. How will it look if you do not marry him? It is widely known in the county that there exists an understanding between you and Mr Keeling. It would be ruinous of your reputation if you were to break the agreement."

"That is impossible. We have never discussed an understanding. He has never spoken of it and nor have I. How can there be an understanding, if I do not know that one exists?"

"There does not have to be an understanding in existence for it to be assumed that there is one, spoken or not. Can you consider how it might appear, with you and Mr Keeling having spent so much time in each other's company of late? You have been seen by servants at both houses, by guests, and the local gentry of Yorkshire. I do not like to speak against my employer, but your grandmother has given no indication to anyone that there does not exist an understanding, when asked about it. She wishes it were so, as does the viscount."

Lavinia sat up in the bed, her eyes wide open in shock. "Do tell me that you are not speaking in earnest! How can this be? I hope he has not heard the same news and thought that it was I who wished for it to be so. How can I face him if he thinks that I have feelings for him and that I wish to marry him?"

"You show more concern for his opinion than you do your good name!"

"How can it be otherwise? He and I are not in any way sympathetic to one another, nor do we hold each other in high regard. He has never once asked me anything about myself, and I have exhausted all possible questions regarding his horses, his interests, and his education. I am quite at my wit's end as to what to talk about in his presence, as he never cares to discuss anything else. Why should I be ashamed to think he would consider my feelings for him to be any more than they are, which is as an acquaintance."

"Lavinia, I do not know how to explain this to you, so that it will not cause you any undue distress, but the time for him being considered an acquaintance, is over. The county expects a wedding, as do your grandmother and the viscount. I should say his brother shares the same expectation. If I may be so bold..." she paused and looked into Lavinia's eyes. "You have not had any other offers of marriage – this may be your one chance to escape a lifetime of solitude as a spinster."

"Charlotte, I respect your counsel," Lavinia answered unaffected. "I know that your advice is given from the depth of your tenderness towards me. You understand my plight as a former orphan and daughter of a village seamstress. However, you must understand what I am trying to say. How can I make you see that there has been no offer of marriage – not even a hint that he should feel in any way romantic towards me?"

"Are you quite certain?" Charlotte asked, her voice calm and even – its tone soothing to Lavinia. "You are young, and you have no experience in matters of love and matrimony. I wish that I was you. I would like to cast off my curse as a spinster and find a way to become a wife one day. I wish the same for you... that you should have a house of your own and children to raise."

"I am touched by your feelings for me. How dear a friend you are, but it does nothing to change my own opinion of Mr Keeling and his lack of regard for me. If we were to marry, I think it would be a terrible mistake. His father would be well-pleased and so would my grandmother, but that would be the end of it. No-one else would share their contentment, least of all me and him."

"Lavinia, if what you have said is true, what are you to do?"

"Can I feign illness and quietly leave Brigham Park?" Lavinia asked hopefully.

"Perhaps, if we had arrived before any of the other guests. However, we have been seen by far too many people to effect a successful escape. Besides, your grandmother is already downstairs in the drawing room playing cards with some of her closest friends. We are far too entrenched here to extricate ourselves at this late hour."

"How many days are we to remain? Two or three? I have never understood these parties. Why must the host insist that we stay imprisoned upon his estate to play cards, dine, and dance?" Lavinia groaned.

Charlotte laughed, "Imprisoned? How very odd you are. I doubt anyone of wealth and rank would consider time spent in the company of other wealthy people, to be as a prison. Only you, Lavinia, could devise such a comparison."

"It is how I feel at this very moment. If only there was a way for me to leave, to run down the servants' stairs, out of the garden, and through the courtyard. I should walk back to Claxton Hall, if I thought I could make the journey in one single night."

"You should take care not to talk like that; you are nearly raving. It is dangerous to be on the moors after dark. I know there are no longer wolves about, but I have heard tales of ferocious beasts on the prowl. If the beasts did not attack you, you might fall prey to highwaymen or, worse yet, a band of gypsies!"

"Charlotte, you have an imagination that is wasted by your being my companion. If you are not married by the time you are well into your thirtieth year, then you should become a writer of novels. Beasts, highwaymen, and gypsies! I would brave all of them, if it meant that I would never have to face Mr Keeling again. If I believed that he thought I wanted to marry him, I would perish from the shame of it."

"Perish or not, I fear he may already know of such gossip. Perhaps, for your sake, he is being a gentleman, and has dismissed such talk as the idle chit chat of women and servants."

"I hope so, for my sake," Lavinia said as she walked to the window.

Her bedroom was a large cold room, located inside a round tower. The floors were of stone, the walls were of the same grey rock, and the tapestries were embroidered in deep shades of crimson and gold that matched the bed curtains. It was a room filled with history and magic, or so she would have thought if she was only a guest of the viscount. While she was a guest, she knew that the reason for her presence inside the house, was not as the ordinary granddaughter of a local wealthy lady, but as the prospective wife of Mr Keeling.

It was because of that same realisation that she strode purposefully towards the window. Staring out into the courtyard, she looked down and saw that the ground below was three or four storeys down. She sized up her chances of escape and decided that there was no way for her to leap out of the window.

She needed to accept her fate. For a brief moment, she wished she was a bird, so that she could fly far away.

Chapter 7

Lavinia was spared the indignation of facing Mr Keeling for more than a brief conversation that first night following their arrival. With a large party of important guests, Mr Keeling, his father, and his older brother, were unable to devote much time to socialising with any guests in particular. Lavinia and Charlotte chose to spend their time in the company of Mrs Talridge and the younger members of her social circle. Sir William Applegate was in attendance, as was his wife and eldest unmarried daughter, Jane. She was a beauty, but what she possessed in lovely features, she lacked in accomplishments. She was dreadful at playing music, her singing voice was regrettable, and she lost nearly every hand of cards she played. Jane was grateful to have Lavinia and Charlotte at her side, as she often said, since they did not take advantage of her terrible luck at the card table.

Amongst the guests at the house, were more nobility than Lavinia had ever seen in one place. Along with the usual assortment of local gentry were two earls, a baronet, and another viscount and his wife. The aristocrats tended to flock together like chickens in a yard – an observation that caused Charlotte and Jane to squeal in shocked delight as they noted the separation of the classes, even amongst the wealthy. Lavinia was feeling the pressure of being the sole commoner amongst the upper-class members of the party, but she did not have time to dwell upon that thought, as she made every effort to be in the company of either Charlotte or Jane, so that Mr Keeling would not find a moment to speak to her. If she could find some way to separate herself from him completely, to be no more pleasant than any of the other guests, then perhaps he would not gaze at her with those green eyes of his – the knowledge that she wanted to marry him making him even more arrogant and conceited.

At her age, she was not entirely certain that she wished to become a wife, but he was, potentially, the only chance she might ever have. How was she supposed to act? Was she supposed to pursue the relationship, content that she was to be married and unable to alter that state once it was done? Or should she do all that she could to promote the feeling in Mr Keeling that she had no wish to be wed to him? She was far more concerned by any suggestion that she wanted to marry him, than she was to have her reputation ruined by the scandal of a failed understanding. If Charlotte was correct, Lavinia had not shown the slightest indication of interest publicly. Perhaps Mr Keeling thought she did not wish to marry him? If she could deter him with coldness in her demeanour, perhaps she could be free of the entire scheme.

A glance across the crowded drawing room showed her that her plans were likely to meet with failure. The viscount was staring at her. With a nod of his head, he offered a weak smile.

Sighing, Lavinia had a terrible suspicion that her fate was no longer her own. What a terrible prospect, when she considered the joy her grandmother felt because of the match. Mrs Talridge sat proudly, her face as beatific as any saint. It would be terrible for her, and her ambitions, if Lavinia did not wed Mr Keeling. Could she break her grandmother's heart after everything the woman had done for her? Lavinia looked at her with a smile so warm and genuine, and the old lady smiled happily back at her. How could she choose to do anything but make her only family happy?

After the last course, the ladies retired to the drawing room, and the men remained in the dining room to drink their brandy. Lavinia did not wish to think any more about her dilemma. Slipping away from the other women, she tried to recall the exact location of the library. She desperately needed solace, but the evening was far from over. If she could find a few moments of peace, she might be able to return to the drawing room in a far better state of mind. Walking quietly down the hallway, she soon realised that she was rather lost. This house was enormous, with its long corridors and dark shadows.

Feeling alone in the house, she listened for any sign that a servant or footman may be about, as she stood in the hallway trying to retrace her steps. She thought she had taken a left turn and then two right turns when the sound of footsteps echoed through the hallway. She felt an enormous feeling of relief as she realised she was no longer alone in the gloom.

Turning to face whoever was coming towards her, she prepared a story to explain why she had become separated from the party. It was not the custom of upper-class women to go roaming about the houses of their hosts, especially at night. Deciding that her adventure to find the library had been folly, she decided to return to the drawing room immediately.

As she peered into the shadows, she expected to see a footman or perhaps a maid, but instead she recognised the face and stature of the gentleman who emerged from the shadows. Mr Keeling was approaching her and there was not a chaperone in sight. It was improper to be alone with a gentleman in brightly lit rooms, how terribly scandalous would it be to be alone with him in the dark of a poorly lit corridor?

"Miss Talridge, was it your intention to pray?" he asked her as he stopped a few feet in front of her.

"Pray?" she asked as she was suddenly thankful for the darkness. The deep and foreboding gloom concealed her embarrassment at being found by the one man she had actively avoided all evening.

"I presume that is your reason for seeking out the chapel after dinner. Are you a pious woman? You do not strike me as the sort to spend your days in prayer."

"Mr Keeling, I do wish that you would speak plainly. Whether I am pious or not, is of little consequence. Can you direct me to the drawing room, please? I seem to have become lost."

"I noticed that you took your leave of the other ladies, without so much as a word to any of your companions."

"Is that why you followed me? Is that proper behaviour for a host?" she asked, aware that she was still very near to him and even more aware that he had been observing her.

Mr Keeling did not reveal any emotions or embarrassment as he replied, "You are a guest of this house. It is my responsibility to see that you do not come to any harm."

"Harm? What harm could befall me in this great house of yours?"

"Miss Talridge, I am sure you are aware of it, but you are approaching one of the oldest parts of this house. You are standing outside the chapel, one of the first rooms in the keep. There has been considerable work done, in recent weeks, to restore the ceilings in the halls and rooms of this section. In the light of day, it is easily manageable to avoid the workers' scaffolding and tools in the corridors, but in the dark of the evening, I dare say that you may have fallen. Please allow me to escort you back to the company of the other ladies," he said as he held out his arm to her.

"I am moved that you were concerned for my safety. I would like to return to the drawing room before it is discovered that I am missing... I was being foolish... I should never have left the others," she admitted.

"You may have been foolish, but I do understand the need to seek out places that are quiet," he said.

Placing her hand on his arm, she felt a slight change in her opinion of him. He was still as emotionless and dutiful as ever, but he had sought her out. His concern for her well-being was touching. In the quiet of the hallway, she whispered, "Would it be too much trouble to view the chapel, even for a moment?"

"The chapel? But it is night. Whatever could you hope to observe? The windows are amongst the finest examples of early stained glass in this part of England. Their beauty can only be appreciated during the day."

"I understand, but I wish to see it anyway, perhaps you could grant me this request?" she asked.

"We cannot tarry, I am afraid, Miss Talridge. There are countless rumours about already. If we are found missing, there will be more."

Lavinia sighed, "You have heard the rumours, I suppose?"

"I have heard them. What causes so many people to care about the private affairs of anyone of property and wealth, I cannot understand."

"Nor can I. Do you dismiss the rumours you have heard?" she asked as she opened the wooden door of the chapel.

Her boldness and determination to see the chapel seemed to evoke a small smile on his lips.

"I do dismiss them, and I suggest you do the same. It would be imprudent to believe everything that you hear." He reached out to the door and held it open for her.

Lavinia understood what he meant. He was telling her that he did not take stock in the rumours and neither should she. It seemed that she and Mr Keeling were the only two people who did not fervently wish to see themselves wed.

As they walked inside the chapel she gasped in awe, forgetting the rumours.

The chapel was larger than she had expected. It was a long, narrow room, with dark wooden pews on either side. High above, the ceiling was vaulted, as in the dining room, only here its stone masonry was more ornate. It reminded her of the older churches and sketches of medieval cathedrals that she had seen in her studies. At the opposite end of the room was a raised dais, and an altar set inside a rounded bay. The windows that were set above the altar must be truly breathtaking in the sunlight. The designs were primitive but consisted of glass in many shades and hues. The reason she had gasped, however, was because of the awe she felt at noticing the wonderful moonlight. The moon had to have been nearly full and moonlight streamed in through the windows, softly illuminating the chapel in the gloom. The light fell on the alter creating a vignette that was truly extraordinary in its mystical simplicity.

"How beautiful!" she whispered as she approached the altar.

"It is," Mr Keeling whispered as she made her way down the aisle.

"If it is this beautiful at night, how must it be during the day?" she wondered.

"We almost lost this whole wing to a fire ten years ago. My father spent an enormous sum to restore it to its previous glory, but it was worth every penny it has taken to keep this place intact. We were fortunate the glass survived."

The sound of his voice, describing the fire and the restoration in the chapel, was soothing. She could hear it in the way he spoke about this room, this place, that this was something he cared about deeply. Gone were the detachment and the disinterest she had observed in the man so many times. Mr Keeling did have sentimental feelings.

"You care about this part of the house, don't you?" she asked, surprised by her own courage.

"I do care about it... you could describe my feelings for it in that manner if you wished. This chapel meant a great deal to my mother." A new smile covered his lips as he looked at her. Was there a sparkle in his eyes?

There was a moment in the stillness of the chapel that did not need to be broken by the sound of words. As she stood silently, feeling the presence of countless generations of Keelings who would have come to the chapel to pray, she realised that while he did not show any indication of caring for the history of his family's house, he did care for his family. He was, therefore, capable of emotions after all, but she suspected that they were concealed deeply within him.

"I do not wish to interrupt your reverie, but we have to be going. The guests will miss us if we do not hurry," he said a few moments later, with a rather cold voice.

Lavinia was shocked at how quickly he returned to his former ways but did not broker any objection.

Leaving the chapel behind, they walked in complete silence back to the drawing room. Mr Keeling had returned to his detached demeanour as easily as she returned to her former opinion of him. *He may be capable of more emotions than she had originally presumed*, she thought, but she realised with a slight pain in her heart, that he was never to be the romantic hero she might have very much wished for.

Chapter 8

The brief interlude at the chapel was nearly forgotten as Lavinia stood beside Charlotte in the ballroom of Brigham Park. Musicians struck a jaunty tune, and she was both afraid, and expected that Mr Keeling would ask her to dance. Lavinia did not understand why he had returned once again to his previous indifferent behaviour towards her. More than that, it suddenly seemed much worse than disinterest; it was the chill of one who was condescending in his nature.

She was pondering the thought, when Charlotte whispered to her, "Jane will surely dance every dance tonight. See how she draws the attention of the gentlemen. She may not be talented in the matters of music and whist, but is there a more glamorous woman in the room?"

Lavinia replied, her disgust evident, "I wonder why the viscount does not choose her as a bride for his son? She seems far more suited, as she is the daughter of a knight. They seem to be a respectable family, from what my grandmother says, and they own a considerable amount of property."

"Sir Applegate owns property, but it is entailed to his son. Jane shall have to find her own way. I do not wish to gossip, but she has said that her annuity is not very generous, the poor dear. It is not nearly as generous as yours," replied Charlotte.

"If it were in my power to give her every last penny of my annuity, to be free of Mr Keeling, I would happily return to Cotes Cross. Have you seen his lack of amity towards me? Except for a brief moment, which I must have completely misjudged, he is now even more disagreeable than he was when we were introduced. I do not want to embarrass my grandmother, but I have no wish to stay another minute here at Brigham Park, nor do I wish to spend one more evening with Mr Keeling."

"Lavinia, you do not mean that."

"I do mean that, and I grow weary of pretending to care about his stable filled with horses. I am bored of polite conversation. How many times have I inquired about his interests or his pursuits when he barely shows the slightest care for me? Do not trouble yourself with an explanation for his boorishness. You have supplied me with a plentiful amount of tedious excuses on his behalf, but where is his excuse, his apology? Is he so proud that he is not capable of admitting even a modest amount of humility, when he wrongs me without the slightest regard?"

Charlotte's brow furrowed as she said, her voice small, "I did not realise you regarded my attempts to explain the manners of his rank as tedious."

In the ballroom with its lovely music and joyful cacophony of laughter, applause, and other sounds of merriment, Lavinia could barely hear her companion's words. To Lavinia's shame, the hurt and pain that Charlotte wore as an expression on her countenance, was unmistakable.

"I did not mean to sound callous towards you, dear Charlotte. It is not your excuses that I find to be tedious. I am vexed with him... cross and filled with the hopelessness of my situation. Forgive me. It is not *you* who should bear my vexation, it is *him*. If he were to admire me even a little... or if he were to regard me as fondly as he does his steed, then I should be content, but he shall never see me as anything other than a woman he was compelled to wed. If I am to speak with candour, I expect that he takes no joy in this match and neither do I. I wish he would direct his displeasure towards his father and leave me alone."

"I'm beginning to understand you. The way he looks at you has not escaped me today." Lavinia's face brightened as Charlotte sighed and showed understanding, "It is *my* fault. I am to blame, and I have been tedious, I am sure of it. You have explained the circumstances of your meetings with him, and I have been too enamoured with the match to accept your opinion. Perhaps there is truth to what you have to say and perhaps he *is* terrible..." she took a moment to take a breath. "A gentleman of worth would not treat a lady as he has treated you, regardless of the difference in rank. You have been accepted into society, you have the full support and acceptance of your grandmother, and your place amongst decent people should not be questioned. You have carried yourself as a lady, and you have never tarnished your reputation with scandal or ruinous behaviour. He owes you the respect of your station – that much at least."

"Oh Charlotte, I was never treated as a villain, even when I did not possess a penny. If I held him in esteem or required a match for my living, I might not feel the pain of his slight in the same way. I would endure him and his temperament as a necessity if I wished to be his wife. As I have no other prospects – other than marriage and spinsterhood – and as he may be the gentleman to overlook my humble beginnings, I feel that I am compelled to bear his disdain, even though I wish it were otherwise. If it were not for the debt I owe my grandmother for her kindness and generosity, I should be free of Mr Keeling, and free to seek my own happiness."

Charlotte's expression softened as she frowned, "I wanted this match to make you happy, my dear Lavinia. I wanted it so badly that I was thinking of my own reaction, if our circumstances were reversed. I know what it means to have to survive by my wits and the generosity of wealthy employers such as your grandmother. *You* may wish to find your own way, but *I* wish to be settled in a house of my own... and it is because of this view that I chose to see your future with Mr Keeling. I have been foolish, when you have spoken time and time again of your displeasure at his inconsiderate treatment."

"Thank you, Charlotte, now you understand. I am in an awful position, and I feel I must accept any proposal, but I do not wish to become his wife. He may be my only hope for a match, but I wish that were not so. What should I do? What can be done for me, to save my grandmother's good name and extricate me from this connection?"

"I am afraid not much can be done. Your grandmother is a singular woman, and she is determined that you will be settled in this great house and attached to this noble family... take heed, here he comes... smile, he is still your host, and you are still Miss Talridge. Do not forget that," Charlotte whispered.

Charlotte and Lavinia bobbed in a curtsy and nodded their heads as Mr Keeling bowed, "Miss Talridge, Miss Fenwick."

"Mr Keeling," Lavinia replied.

"Miss Talridge, it would be an honour if you would dance with me. Have you a place reserved for your host?"

Lavinia's heart beat wildly. She wanted to tell the man that she did not have a place reserved for him, but she felt the uneasy sensation of a room filled with aristocrats and her grandmother's peers staring at her, as obvious as if they were watching a spectacle.

She replied, "I would find dancing with you to be an..."

She fought the temptation to narrow her eyes and finish the sentence with the word "imposition", but she knew that being a young woman of rank held certain expectations. Sighing as she plastered a façade of contentment on her face, she finished her sentence as a proper young woman would, by saying, "...honour, thank you."

How the words she spoke stuck in her throat, as he held out his arm to her! Placing her gloved hand on his outstretched arm, he led her to centre of the room. She did not need to look at her grandmother to know that Mrs Talridge was smiling whilst being congratulated by the bevy of older woman who plotted their daughters' and grand-daughters' future lives behind the doors of drawing rooms and at tea.

The music began, and they danced easily, as did the other couples who joined them. He was light on his feet, he smiled at the appropriate times, and gave her the proper compliments. To both the casual and studied observers of the room, he appeared to be properly attentive to his companion. Many would remark that the couple were well-suited, as they appeared to be beautiful, elegant, and graceful in their movements. However, Lavinia could not ignore the lingering disdain that seemed to lie in the depths of his eyes as he looked at her – that bitter coldness most others did not see, and that she would never accept.

Looking at the other couples who danced, chattered gaily, and enjoyed the opportunity for conversation that dancing afforded them, Lavinia was envious. Even though she smiled, she was thrilled when the tune came to an end. She wanted to make a hasty retreat, far away from Mr Keeling, but that was not to be. At the subtle beckoning of the viscount, Mr Keeling led Lavinia towards his father.

The Viscount of Wharton stood as resolute as a stone statue. His posture was rigid, and his eyes were set in a reserved expression. Only his lips turned up in a smile that expressed a sentiment that seemed to be at odds with the remaining features of his face. Lavinia was familiar with the expression, as she had seen it mirrored on Mr Keeling's face when he made the slightest attempt to treat her with anything other than obvious contempt.

"Miss Talridge, are you enjoying the hospitality of Brigham Park?" the viscount asked Lavinia.

Uncertain of what to say other than to proffer the expected response, she said, "Lord Wharton, your hospitality has been generous, and I thank you for the invitation."

The viscount continued, "Has my son paid you proper attention, seeing that you have enjoyed your time here at this house?"

The words "No, not at all" reigned inside Lavinia's mind as she tried to grasp the intentions of the viscount. It was not his custom to engage in conversation with her, or to do anything other than to observe her from a distance.

Carefully measuring her words, she responded, "He has behaved as an intent host, and I have found Brigham Park to be much more than I expected."

To Lavinia's surprise, the viscount did not waste any time on subtleties and nuances but instead, he came directly to the reason for his interest in speaking with her. "That is splendid. Then you are well acquainted with the idea of a match between yourself and my son? Your grandmother has informed me that you are pleased with him."

Lavinia was unable to answer, as she struggled to formulate the proper sentiment for disagreeing with a man as intimidating and imposing as the viscount. She was disgusted by his ill-treatment of the villagers of Cotes Cross, which made her naturally predisposed towards dislike and distrust. In this moment, she wished to express her repulsion of the idea that she would be pleased to marry Mr Keeling, but before she could respond in her own right, he chose to join the conversation as more than a silent witness.

"Father, there is no need to have this discussion at the ball. Perhaps another, less public time would be more suitable?" said Mr Keeling.

"George, there will be no further discussion. The matter is concluded. I will announce your engagement to Miss Talridge, this very evening."

The calm manner in which the Viscount of Wharton spoke the sentence that would alter Lavinia's future, beyond her control, sickened her. To a powerful man such as the viscount, her feelings, even if she dared to express them, would mean nothing. His pretence of polite interest in her sentiments for his son, was as much a facade as his smile. She was the living that his son would earn; she was no more than a way to acquire a portion of Mrs Talridge's fortune.

"Father," Mr Keeling began.

"There will be no further discussion," the viscount replied as he gazed at Lavinia in a manner that made her nervous.

"Miss Talridge," the viscount remained undaunted by Mr Keeling's apparent disgust and Lavinia's expression of shock as he spoke – as emotionless as one who might be engaged in a negotiation regarding livestock or timber. "I suspect that you are not offended by the manner in which you have come by your happiness. You and my son may discuss the details that all young couples talk of... If you require romance, he may ask you for your hand if you wish, but the matter has been concluded. Your grandmother was generous, and there shall be nothing further said on the matter."

Mrs Talridge had been as generous with Lavinia as if she were her own daughter and not some poor relation. She had done all that was right and good by Lavinia, but at this moment, it was impossible for her to be appreciative of her grandmother's generosity.

Lavinia was not prepared for the proposal to be delivered by Mr Keeling's father, nor was she prepared to endure it with grace.

Lavinia sought escape.

She longed to run from the room, out of Brigham Park and far away. She looked around the room like a captured beast crazed and panicked for release. Her heart beat hard within her chest, her breathing was shallow, and she was nearly faint with fright. She must leave, she must take flight – but there was no escape.

Her grandmother smiled benevolently from across the room. The room drew close and the walls seemed to close in on her as she tried to steady her nerves. She could not faint, not in front of the viscount or Mr Keeling. Unable to ignore the jubilant expression on her grandmother's face, Lavinia did not smile back. Instead, her face was as hard as stone when their eyes met. Mrs Talridge's smile slipped, revealing a look of troubled concern that was fleeting.

Her fate wrapping around her like a trap, Lavinia's knees began to buckle. She reached out desperately for Mr Keeling's arm – a necessary evil as she endeavoured to remain conscious. She found his arm frozen and hard, and his eyes equally so, as he looked at her with un-mitigated bitterness. The look she saw on his face was terrible and one she swore she would never forget.

Chapter 9

"George, you should take care that you do not earn a reputation for eccentricity... If the staff think that you have become odd, their gossip shall soon spread amongst all the great houses of the county. How will I answer for your strange behaviour?" Denton teased his brother as he leaned casually against the wall of the stable inside a stall, which was an unusual place for the heir to Brigham Park. A man of his wealth and property would ordinarily be found inside the great stone residence, sitting near a fire with a brandy in his hand.

Hard rain pelted against the roof of the stable and the horses neighed their displeasure in their stalls, expressing their discontent at the sudden storm. In a dark mood, George dismissed the stable boys and groomsmen and brushed his horse himself, his hair dripping from the rain and his clothes drenched.

"Odd, am I? Eccentric? So, what if I am? What do I care for the gossip of servants any more than I care for the gossip of old women?" George replied.

"George, I am your brother. It has been a fortnight since the ball... and father is furious. Personally, I do not mind if you want to be as mad as you like, but I do wish you would reconsider this display until *after* your marriage."

George stared at his brother in a manner that was intended to indicate his disgust. "Marriage? If you find her to be suitable, why are you not wed to her already?"

"Be reasonable brother, I am the next viscount and *my* marriage will be decided on rank and fortune. I wish I might find a lady as interesting as Miss Talridge. She is unlike any woman of our acquaintance – keen, observant, and she possesses a wit that her companion Miss Fenwick ceaselessly quotes."

"All I want is to be free to join Wellington abroad on the continent."

"Do you still profess a desire to join the army? A marriage to Miss Talridge will bring you a comfortable annuity, secure your future, and ensure that you possess as many horses as you could ever desire."

George patted the horse with gentleness, and turned to face his brother, "What do I care for the annuity that Miss Talridge possesses? Did you not listen?"

"Father is satisfied with the arrangement, as I hoped you would be. I admit that your future will not be as grand as if you were the elder of us, but you will do very well for a younger brother," Denton said as calmly as he could.

"I wish to do *more* than marry, to suit the whims of father or to secure an income for myself. There is a war going on, in case you have not been informed, and that war continues and seems to have no end in sight. There can be no victory over Napoleon and his forces, if men who are born to lead, do nothing but sit idly by. I repeat, why must I be satisfied with a marriage, simply to suit the avarice of my father? If *he* wants a portion of Mrs Talridge's wealth and if *he* wants to ensure that I have an income, why must *I* accept this match? What makes this match far more favourable than a commission in the army?"

"He favours this match because it is satisfactory, considering your position."

"My position?" George snorted, his disgust no longer concealed, "If father will not permit me to join the army, why does he insist that I accept a woman to be my wife? It is insufferable that I should not be allowed to go where I may be of use leading a regiment to aid Wellington instead of this arrangement."

Denton looked at his brother as if he was unable to grasp a simple concept. "Brother! What has gotten into you in these last few weeks – I hardly recognise you. Has father not explicitly explained it to you? You shall not be allowed to join Wellington, not when your future is in question, and not when a match has been made. There is no market for second sons amongst the women of our own class, and if there is such a match, it is surely the exception."

"If it is an exception, then why can I not serve? Cannot Miss Talridge, or whoever I am forced to wed for the sake of my father's mercenary interest, wait until I return from the army?"

Looking up towards the ceiling of the stables, Denton spoke absentmindedly of the subject. "Are you certain you wish to join Wellington for the reasons you have mentioned, for honour and the service of the realm? Is that the reason, or do you find the continent to be an exciting escape from the monotony of your life?"

"Denton, I have not wavered in my desire to serve, not once, and it is father who has shown no interest in hearing my desire to be of use. He would rather see me unhappily wed than do my duty, and that is the source of my frustration. My life will be forfeit in an arranged match, rather than sacrificed on the field of honour. As a gentleman and a Keeling, how am I to live my life, knowing that I accepted those circumstances?"

George's brother looked at him firmly. "Miss Talridge is a fine young woman. You need to be a gentleman in this matter and understand the duty of your station, George. If you cannot bear to respect the woman who will be your wife, some respect for her grandmother is due. Mrs Talridge may not come from as storied a lineage as your own, but she has done nothing to earn your contempt. I dare say you deserve to be in the army, amongst men who know nothing but the manners of the battlefield rather than that of a drawing room. Certainly, if you are going to regard women who are above reproach, in this manner," Denton chastised his younger brother.

George was unremorseful, as he replied, "This match can bring me no honour and no comfort."

"Comfort or not, the announcement has been made, and your plans of joining Wellington are at an end. You will be wed to Miss Talridge by Christmas, although I suspect you may be her husband at an earlier date if her grandmother has her way."

"Denton, Father does not leave me with any options that are honourable. I do not wish to involve you in any action that would bring his anger upon you, but I cannot marry Miss Talridge," insisted George.

Denton was quiet for a couple of moments and when he began to speak, he seemed to have lost patience.

"The storm is getting worse. If we do not go inside soon, we may catch our death of cold and wet – and then it will not matter what your or my future holds."

"Denton, I am entirely serious," George insisted.

"Shall I speak to father on your behalf?"

"There is no need, as he does not listen to me, and I doubt he will listen to you. There is nothing to be done except what I must."

Denton was silent again, appearing to no longer be listening as he walked out of the stall, leaving his younger brother alone with his horse.

George shivered, and his wet clothes clung to him as he contemplated his fate. What a waste for his death to be as ignoble as the result of illness or a cold bed as a husband. His death should count for something on the fields of France. Why did his father and his brother not see it with the same clarity that he did?

Chapter 10

"Is she not eating? This makes it the third time this week." Mrs Talridge said to Charlotte.

"She claims that she isn't hungry. Shall I see that she is dressed for dinner and ordered to join us at the table?"

"No, that won't be necessary. I will see that her dinner is sent up on a tray," Mrs Talridge replied. "I do wish I understood what has taken her appetite. When I was a bride, I did not suffer from conditions or ailments of the nerves…"

"Mrs Talridge, if I may offer my judgement. I know it is not my place to offer any disagreement with you, as I respect your opinion, but I feel that you have not fully given Lavinia's condition the proper consideration. Forgive me for my insolence, but Lavinia has never shown any previous inclination towards nervous ailments, and as her companion and former governess, I do not attribute her present condition to any cause other than her impending nuptials. Her constitution is not weak, nor is she the fragile sort."

Frowning, Mrs Talridge replied, "Perhaps I shall see how she fares, after we have dined. I think it would be best if I were to form my own opinion about what may be the cause of her malady. It will never do to have her illness become known. If it were publicly speculated that she is sickly and weak, the viscount may reconsider a marriage to his son… No-one wants a woman who will be forever prone to illnesses, and therefore of no use at all."

Upstairs in her bed, Lavinia lay under the covers. She was dressed in her night shirt and her hair fell in a braid down her back. The sun had set two hours ago, as the late autumn evening brought darkness at an early hour. Her wedding day was nearly upon her, and she could find no comfort except in lying in her bed.

The dinner tray lay untouched on a table beside the fireside as the wind howled against the windows. Outside the temperature was cold, and inside her room she felt a chill that was from neither the weather nor from an ailment.

Since the announcement of her engagement, Mr Keeling appeared at her side only as often as was required. He made no attempt to hide his real feelings, even though he smiled and did what was expected of a suitor. He seemed as resigned to their shared fate as she was, even though neither of them had openly discussed it in a meaningful way – *except during their moment in the chapel*, she thought to herself as she stared at the candle, flickering in its holder on her bedside table.

A knock at the door announced the arrival of the maid for the dinner tray. Lavinia barely noticed the door open or the sound of footsteps crossing the floor, until she was suddenly faced with a person who was not the maid.

"Lavinia, this is intolerable. You have not touched your dinner... you look pale, and you have grown thin and wan. I will not have it. If you are truly suffering from an ailment, I shall send for the apothecary and if that will not do, then the doctor will be summoned," her grandmother said as she placed a hand on Lavinia's forehead. "If you do not show the slightest indication that you are unwell, then you shall have to alter your behaviour at once, because it is intolerable that you should behave so diabolically this close to your wedding,"

She took her hand away from Lavinia's forehead.

"It is as I suspected," she said as she peered at Lavinia, "You are not ill. Instead, you are suffering from no more than a nervous condition. I insist that you refrain from exhibiting any more demonstrations of this foolishness. What will people think? Here you are, about to be wed to a Keeling. You are the luckiest girl in the county, and you insist on this behaviour!"

"Grandmother, it is not that I am being stubborn... It is you who are being incapable of altering your opinion. I do not wish to be ungrateful, but the only malady I suffer, is that of not wanting to be wed to Mr Keeling. I thought I could force myself to do my duty to you, but I cannot. I just cannot."

"Are you lying in your bed as a spoiled child would? Is this how you intend to repay my kindness, by embarrassing me?"

"I do not wish to embarrass you. I thought I could bring myself to accept him as a husband and to do my duty to you. I have never wished to act in any way other than as a reflection of my loyalty to you, as your kindness has been boundless. I know that I owe all that I am and all that I have to you."

Mrs Talridge softened, as she sat on the edge of Lavinia's bed. "If you are aware of your duty, then you should not act as you do. What will happen if it becomes known that you are against this match?"

"It would be fortunate if it should become known, considering that I was never consulted about Mr Keeling."

"Not consulted?" Mrs Talridge said in a huff.

"You and the viscount decided on the match. I was informed by the viscount, and then it was announced. If you force me to marry him, I will have no other choice... but I dislike Mr Keeling – and he loathes me."

"What an imagination you have. He does *not* loathe you, child. And what do you mean you were not consulted? I find the idea preposterous. Of course, you were!"

"I was told by you what I should think of him and the family. Grandmother, I was informed that I should find myself lucky to be marrying into that family. You did not ask me if I wanted to marry him, nor did Mr Keeling!" Lavinia exclaimed, her voice echoing loudly in her room.

"Do not raise your voice to me, Lavinia. You show not the slightest regard for my efforts to purchase you a name and a connection," her grandmother said as she rose to her feet. Her face arranged itself into a scowl. "Regarding the matter of a consultation on the subject of Mr Keeling – why should I ask you? What opinion would you give me that would be of any use? Are you my age? Do you have the slightest understanding of the world, or of what you face as a woman without a husband or family to stand beside you? I have ensured that your future is secure and that you shall never be in need, nor know want for the reminder of your days. If I did not ask you, if Mr Keeling did not propose, it is of no consequence. Your life will be far better than the prospects of your companions, or what they may have been, had I left you in Cotes Cross!"

"I wish that you had left me there. Look at Mr Keeling, truly look at him. See how he regards me with ill-concealed hatred. He barely speaks to me and when he is in my presence, his disinterest when I speak is apparent to all who have eyes. Only *you* wish that I should be married to him. You and his father, who regards me as nothing more than my annuity."

"Has he spoken to you about breaking off the match?" Mrs Talridge asked, her concern apparent in her words.

"Is that all you care about... this match? I thought you cared for me," Lavinia cried.

"I do care for you, you silly girl. Oh, you are so young... too young to understand. I will not be in this world all the years of your life. Soon, you will be left with no-one who champions you and Claxton Hall will be inherited by my nephew. You will have your annuity and some money upon my death, but that will be all to sustain you. Without me as your family, as your connection, the unfortunate circumstances of your birth will not be accepted by very many people of polite society, and you will find no welcome or warmth anywhere."

"I shall return to Cotes Cross. I will find a modest dwelling and set up for myself if I shall be expelled from proper society," Lavinia said defiantly.

Mrs Talridge appeared stricken as she strode across the room, leaving Lavinia defiant and unapologetic. Turning to face her granddaughter, she sighed, her shoulders hunched in exhaustion as she said, "It matters not if you return to Cotes Cross or if you live anywhere in the country. Who shall be your friends, who shall you seek for company? You are educated, and you will most likely find the company of the common people tedious. You will be unwelcome to those of worth. It is a lonely existence that awaits you, if you do not accept my aid. I do not wish for your unhappiness. On the contrary, I have struggled on your behalf, and I have worked very hard to see that you are settled before my death. If that is not a sign of my care for you then what pray tell, is?"

Lavinia was alone in her room after her grandmother left. Finding sleep to be of little comfort, she lay in her bed or paced the floor in front of the fireplace, her thoughts disturbed. She was so certain of her right to be angry and vexed at her grandmother for putting her in this terrible predicament, but as she considered her grandmother's words, and remembered the look of hurt on the older woman's face, Lavinia felt worse than foolish. She saw her actions from the perspective of her grandmother. Mrs Talridge had before never spoken so plainly of Lavinia's prospects, nor what would happen to her in society without her support.

Lavinia's predicament was far worse than she knew.

While she had presumed that her parentage would cause her some difficulty in finding a husband, she had not understood the true direness of her circumstances until that very night. Her grandmother was a woman of class and great reserve, and she spoke her mind, but never at the expense of decorum. For her to have spoken the truth, in its unveiled plainness, told Lavinia about what motivated her fears. It was an unprecedented moment and Lavinia regarding it as chilling. She had dreamed of finding her own way in the world, and of living a life according to her dictates. If she found a husband, she wished for a gentleman or at the very least a man who adored her. Now, she understood with perfect clarity that she no longer fit into the world of her youth and finding a husband without her grandmother's support would be dreadfully difficult.

When she thought of how terribly she had treated her grand-mother; how she had misunderstood her, she felt guilty. Her grand-mother had looked hurt by her callous words and by her lack of grati-tude. How could Lavinia be so wrong about her grandmother? She had thought the woman was enamoured of a connection to the Keel-ing family and that she had a romantic notion of what a match be-tween Lavinia and Mr Keeling could be. Now Lavinia understood that all Mrs Talridge wished to do was to make certain that Lavinia was well placed, when she no longer had her grandmother to stand by her side.

In her own way, her grandmother was giving Lavinia a secure fu-ture, even though she was unwilling or unable to see that the future for Lavinia was less appealing when it came attached to Mr Keeling.

By the early hours of the morning, Lavinia had slept very little of the night. She yawned and contemplated lying in the bed for a few more hours, but she knew that it would be a futile attempt. She had decided on a solution to her dilemma. After she had dressed for the day with-out the assistance of her maid, she sat on the chaise-longue beside the fire, warming her hands while she waited for the appointed hour when her grandmother would appear downstairs.

She rushed past the oil paintings of the corridor and stopped at one she knew well. It was a painting of a young man and his horse.

The man was painted astride a tall coal-black horse with a black mane. He was sitting on the horse wearing an expression of absolute dominance over all that he surveyed. In the painting, he was seated in the saddle with the rolling hills of the Claxton Hall estate surrounding him. Lavinia knew this painting well – it was her father. She found the likeness to be tragic, and yet she was drawn to the painting. He was young, and his confidence in his world and his life, was evident. The painter had captured his countenance in remarkable detail – how her father was capable of love and compassion, and capable of loving her mother, who was a commoner. How had he come by his extraordinary capacity for love? When she thought of her grandmother, she knew the answer. Her grandmother was acting in the only way that one who is motivated by love, does. Lavinia could feel her grandmother's love, and she could feel the woman's fears for her and her future.

Lavinia knew then that she would find a way to reconcile herself to her marriage with Mr Keeling. She would not marry him just to set her grandmother's mind at ease. She would make her grandmother proud by trying to find some sort of agreement with him, to make the best of the situation. Should he, after the marriage, continue treating her coldly, then she would seek her own place in his household and endeavour to carve out a life for herself without him or his presence, living her life as she saw fit (or at least as much as she could, as a married woman).

With Mr Keeling equally as unenthusiastic about the match, she doubted he would offer any objections to her actions, or care one whit for what she did, provided she had nothing to do with him.

She knew she would never love him, and she wholeheartedly doubted that he would ever seek to earn her love, but maybe he would one day open up to her as he had that evening in the chapel. Maybe she would come to learn his motives, so that they could find a way to overcome this great hurdle that had been placed upon them and find a way to live harmoniously together. Lavinia thought of the good works she could accomplish as the wife of a Keeling, where she would be in a position to do even more for the people – the ill, and the poor.

Yes, she decided, she would go downstairs and ask her grandmother's forgiveness, and she would make amends.

Chapter 11

"My word, Lavinia, you look beautiful," Charlotte whispered as she adjusted Lavinia's dress.

Lavinia did not say anything to her friend about the marriage, if only to calm her own set of nerves. As Lavinia was becoming a bride, she would have no further need for a governess, a tutor, or a companion. Charlotte had expressed concern that she should advertise for a new position, but Mrs Talridge had told her it was entirely unnecessary, as she had already made it clear that she wished to engage Charlotte Fenwick as her own companion, after Lavinia's wedding.

"What will you do without me to vex you and cause you concern? Will you be comfortable as my grandmother's companion when I am married?" Lavinia asked.

"I will be comfortable, although I will miss you terribly. Your grandmother was very gracious in not making me search for another situation, and I feel as much at home at Claxton Hall as I have ever been, anywhere. It grieves me to know that one day I will have to leave it behind."

"We shall not dwell on that now. My grandmother is a strong woman – resilient and vigorous. When I visit here in ten years and more, I will find you both having tea in the drawing room, with my cousin fuming that he cannot yet claim the house," Lavinia said with a giggle.

"I pray that it will be so... I would like nothing more. Are you quite prepared to meet Mr Keeling at the altar?" Charlotte asked under her breath.

Lavinia recalled a conversation, one of several she had had with her closest friend and companion. She had vowed not to disclose the full details of her scheme concerning her marriage to Mr Keeling. However, she did tell her friend a small portion of her plans, explaining her sudden acceptance of the wedding that she had spent so long lambasting. Charlotte was reluctant to understand Lavinia's change in position, but she supported her friend as a true friend would. Charlotte offered her words of comfort and encouragement, congratulating her, even though neither woman truly felt that this was a day that warranted any celebration. In front of the maids and Lavinia's grandmother, she and Charlotte were careful to confine their comments to what would be expected on that day. Her wedding day was supposed to be a joyful event and a day of happiness for Lavinia, as it should be for any young woman.

"My dear, that ivory satin gown is quite becoming. Your dark hair shines against the golden hue of the netting and the veil. I was perfectly correct to order that style of bonnet for your wedding. The colour lends distinct warmth to your features... yes, the ensemble is becoming. I dare say you will be amongst the most charming brides in Yorkshire," Mrs Talridge gushed as she slipped a small, crimson velvet box in Lavinia's hand. "This is for you. It brought good fortune to me upon my wedding day, and it is fitting that you should have it."

Lavinia felt the soft velvet of the tiny crimson box in her fingers. It was trimmed in gold piping that seemed very old. Carefully, she opened the lid to reveal a gold filigree band inlaid with tiny sapphires.

It was dazzling in its simplicity and heavier than she expected. The gold was thick and rounded with age.

"This was my mother's ring, and then it was mine. I give it you to pass on to your eldest daughter, one day." Mrs Talridge explained.

Lavinia felt a twinge of guilt knowing that if her plan succeeded, it was highly unlikely that there would be a daughter. Dismissing all thoughts of her scheme, she tried to tell her grandmother to pass the ring down to her nephew so that it might stay in the family, but she could not say the words. The ring, like her grandmother, was far too beautiful and rare to be overlooked, and she could not say no to her grandmother, nor did she wish to. She removed the ring from its velvet cocoon and slipped it on to the second finger of her right hand, admiring the sparkle of the stones, and fighting back her tears as she did so.

Sniffing, Lavinia said, "Thank you. This ring is lovely, and I will treasure it dearly."

"Soon, you will have so many rings and jewels that you won't recall that you own this ring, but for today it will be with you. You are my granddaughter, and you deserve to wear it," Mrs Talridge said as she patted Lavinia's hand.

"Lavinia, do you have your gloves? Are you ready to meet your groom?" Charlotte asked as she fussed over her friend.

"I am as ready as I can be. Do you think the church will be very crowded? I hope not – I am nervous enough just thinking about what I must say and do."

"Nervous?" her grandmother asked as she smiled. "There is no need to be nervous. I suspect the church is filled with all our neighbours and the society of the Keelings, but that should be of no concern to you. After your wedding, you will find yourself to be the social superior of many of those fine people, and you may dismiss their opinions if you so desire, for all that will matter is that from this day, you shall be Mrs George Keeling."

Lavinia smiled in return, as her grandmother embraced her, kissing her on her cheek. Her grandmother's eyes glistened as she continued, "There you are. You look beautiful. I am convinced that we made the right choice of dressmaker."

Charlotte's eyes were red from the tears that welled up as she added, "Lavinia if I were to be married, I would wish for a pretty dress just like the one you're wearing. There will not be a woman in the church who will not envy you today."

Lavinia listened to their compliments, feeling buoyed by their insistence that she would find herself to be amongst the comeliest of brides. As she had expected, her reflection in the mirror showed her as an upper-class woman, dressed in ivory satin. Her bonnet was adorned with ivory ribbon and a small spray of ivory flowers. She appeared for all the world as a woman who was going to church to meet her destiny, but secretly she knew that today was simply the beginning of her life as a married woman.

Lavinia had been taught that in proper society she should be obedient to her husband, but she doubted Mr Keeling would enforce his will or command of her (she doubted he would say much to her at all).

Smiling as she smoothed the material of her skirt, she looked down at the ring on her finger. She could feel the pride and love of her grandmother when she felt the weight of the band on her finger. Mrs Talridge thought her granddaughter was beginning a new secure part of her life, content and satisfied, but Lavinia knew that today would be the beginning of an adventure and a deceit. If she was fortunate, being married to Mr Keeling would be an inconvenience at best.

Taking a deep breath, Lavinia made an announcement. "I am ready. We shouldn't keep the guests waiting... or Mr Keeling."

Lavinia had scarcely moved from the mirror when a maid appeared at the door to her room. The woman's eyes were wild with fright, and her face was as pale as the dress on Lavinia's back.

"Mrs Talridge, if you please forgive me, but this came for you," the maid said, as she thrust out a folded piece of paper. She lowered herself into a curtsey as she waited for Mrs Talridge to take possession of the slip of paper. "Lord Wharton's man is downstairs in the hall," the maid added as she looked around the room wide-eyed and seemingly uncomfortable.

"How very strange. Why would he have sent a man, unless he has sent his carriage for your use?" Charlotte suggested.

Mrs Talridge unfolded the letter and read the words carefully and slowly under her breath. All colour drained from her face until she was as pale as the maid who stood at her side. Turning the paper over she read every word again and the pallor in her cheeks was supplanted by a deep crimson, as red as the velvet box on Lavinia's dressing table.

"Grandmother, what's the matter?" Lavinia asked, seeing her grandmother's mood transform from jubilance to fury.

"Mrs Talridge?" Charlotte asked, sensing the change in the room.

"Hester," Mrs Talridge addressed the shrinking maid, "Tell the man in the hall to wait for my reply. Everyone, out at once, do you hear me! Out!" Mrs Talridge almost shouted, as she ordered the maids to leave the room.

Charlotte began to walk out of the door behind the staff, but Mrs Talridge reached out for her, shoving the paper into her hand.

Lavinia was overcome with curiosity as to what could account for her grandmother's rapid change of mood. Her grandmother was not the type of woman to go about ordering her domestic staff around in such a terse manner.

Charlotte gasped, and then she repeated Mrs Talridge's exact actions, examining the paper for any trace of further writing. She shook her head, which caused her curls to shake violently as she read the paper, and then she read it again.

"Charlotte, Grandmother, what has happened?" Lavinia could withstand the suspense no longer.

"Lavinia, I do not know what to say," Charlotte began, but then stopped as she looked at Mrs Talridge.

Mrs Talridge was livid.

Her face was red, and her jaw was firmly set as she appeared to be literally shaking with anger. Lavinia could never recall having seen her grandmother as angry as she was at this moment, and she felt frightened and unsure of what to make of the mysterious letter or of her grandmother's violent reaction to it.

"Charlotte, send an urgent message to my solicitor in London. Write to him that I may be in need of his services, if the viscount is not willing to honour his part of the contract in the present circumstances."

"Yes ma'am. What should I say about the present circumstances? Shall I reveal their true nature?" Charlotte asked as her expression turned to one of steely-eyed determination.

"You may enclose a copy of the letter if you wish – include every word. I want him to see it verbatim, but we shall retain the original with its seal, should we have use for it. Dispatch the message immediately. Do not delay." Mrs Talridge demanded in an icy tone.

"Yes ma'am, I will see to it." Charlotte replied as she rushed from the room.

"Grandmother, you have not told me what has happened. Why would you need your solicitor?" Lavinia asked as she pushed the veil away from her face.

"Lavinia, steel yourself for some bad news, my dear." Mrs Talridge said in a tone of voice that did little to conceal the fury that her face betrayed.

Lavinia did as her grandmother commanded. She sat down in the chair at her dressing table. She wrung her hands nervously as she considered what terrible news could have prompted her grandmother to send a message to her solicitor in London.

"My dear, I have some terrible news. I do not know quite how to tell you this, but I shall try to break it to you gently, so that you will not have a shock."

"Tell me. I am ready. What is it?" Lavinia asked, feeling she could no longer wait in suspense. She removed the bonnet from her head as she no longer wished to feel the ribbon tied around her neck.

She felt that the ribbon, like the bonnet, was stifling her, and so were her gloves as her pulse raced. She slid the gloves from her hands, and she could feel her palms sweating in response to her apprehension.

"I am the bearer of the worst news, but it is far better that you hear it from me and not in front of church filled with people... your wedding will not be today, my dear... You are not getting married to Mr Keeling." Mrs Talridge explained in a steady, careful way.

For a moment, there was silence.

"I am not getting married *today*? Is there a cause for the delay?" Lavinia asked, her panic dissipating as she tried to understand what was happening.

"You are not getting married to Mr Keeling today or any other day. He has abandoned his duty to you and to his family. He seems to have left you and left Yorkshire... and I fear he may never return."

Again, silence.

"Mr Keeling has left me on the day we are to wed?"

"According to this letter from his father, he left Brigham Park late last night. He was expected to return, to marry you at the appointed hour, but there has been word that he will not be coming back. There are more details but... my poor dear granddaughter, you must be in shock – shall I send for the apothecary?"

Lavinia stood up, slowly walking to the window of her room. It was nearly Christmas and cold winds blew outside as the first snowfall lay on the dead grass and branches of the garden. Everything was white and serene. Watching the peaceful scenery Lavinia knew she should be mortified that all of her grandmother's friends and acquaintances were assembled at the church, waiting for a wedding that would never be. Her grandmother was furious and stricken with anger, but all

Lavinia could feel was... a sense of relief. She would not be marrying Mr Keeling, not today or any other day. The embarrassment she felt at being discarded, was not nearly as powerful as the astonishment she felt at this turn of events. However, she knew that she could not appear to be relieved, as her grandmother's hopes for her had been so evidently crushed.

Turning to her grandmother, she asked, "Where is Mr Keeling, do you know?"

"No, my dear, I do not know where he is, but I suspect we shall discover the truth in good time. I have to send word to the vicar and to the guests at the church... there is much to be done, but I am anxious for you. Are able to bear this burden?" Mrs Talridge asked as she reached out to her granddaughter, her hand falling on Lavinia's dark curls.

Lavinia looked away from the winter garden and looked deeply into the face of her grandmother. She saw determination and fire in the old woman's eyes. There was resolve and there was anger, both in equal measure. Lavinia said, in a quiet tone of voice, "I wager if he is anywhere at all, you will find him, won't you?"

"Not at all, my dear! I have no wish to ever acknowledge his presence again... but I will discover the reason for this grave insult to your honour – and to my own. This slight will *not* go unmet or unchallenged, but that concern is for me to bear alone. What of you, my dearest Lavinia? What shall be done to ease your sorrow?"

"I am more embarrassed and humiliated than sorrowful," Lavinia confessed.

"Of course! You are a young woman dressed for her wedding, who has been left by her prospective husband! It shows a lack of character and honour that I did not anticipate from the son of a historic and noble family. I will give this matter my full attention, but in the meantime, I shall send Charlotte to you, to ease your loneliness and grief."

Lavinia fell into her grandmother's arms and tears of relief washed over her, and also indignation. She was grateful that she would not be forced to marry the disagreeable man, but she did feel the slight of his actions. It was not only the neglect she felt from Mr Keeling, but a fear had begun to well up inside her.

"Grandmother, did he abandon me because my father and mother were not married? Will I never find a man who will have me as I am, with that blemish of taint upon me?" Lavinia lamented.

"Mark my words. You shall find a good husband. I will make certain of it. Do not allow yourself to dwell on such terrible thoughts. They are my concern, as I have said. Change out of your wedding clothes, but be careful that you do not rend the garment in any way. as we will have use for it."

Lavinia felt better after her grandmother's reassurance. However, the embarrassment was real, and so was the concern for her future. What would she do? As she watched her grandmother leave, she thought of Mr Keeling and wondered briefly where he may have gone if he had abandoned his own family and Yorkshire?

Chapter 12

Spring arrived in Yorkshire, as it always did, with blustery winds, rain storms and a hint of green upon the moors. Lavinia was revived, as were the fields and lawns surrounding Claxton Hall. For the months since Mr Keeling had abandoned her, she and Charlotte had remained at Claxton Hall, at the insistence of her grandmother. She ventured out for church and the occasional tea, but not much else. Mrs Talridge assured her that it was necessary that she should take great care not to appear in public, as that may lead to gossip that she may have been the cause of the disastrous ending of the match. She could not be seen to be enjoying the company of other men, or at the card tables or dinners, as she was the sympathetic character in the opinion of every person in the county.

Lavinia understood the necessity for a quiet winter, away from the social whirl of parties and celebrations. Although she longed for distraction, she knew that her reputation was important, and that she should be seen as the slighted woman. With the coming of spring, she longed to return to her old village, to go visiting, as well as to do a hundred things she had never thought she would miss. Lavinia was astonished that she should desire to be in society, when for so many months before her abandonment at the altar, she had eschewed nearly every social occasion, preferring the company of a book or the solitude of Charlotte or her grandmother's company.

She smiled at her reflection in the mirror of her dressing table, clothed in a soft-blue afternoon frock, as she thought of the afternoon's schedule. The vicar was due for a visit and perhaps Mrs Applegate and her daughter Jane. How Lavinia wished to see familiar faces, and to laugh and smile again!

How quiet Claxton Hall had been these past few months. The snows of winter made travel difficult in Yorkshire. Yet it was not only the weather that had led to a dull winter. Many of the wealthy families had braved the roads south, to London, for the winter season, which made the county a very dull place for a young woman who was bursting to do something (and to hear some news). Lavinia also suspected that the drop in the number of social calls her grandmother made, and indeed the few she received, were the result of the dreadful business with Mr Keeling. Many of the families who did not journey to London, treated the Talridges as though they were in mourning. Lavinia supposed it must have seemed that way, as her grandmother engineered that very appearance.

With her hair curled and pinned into place, Lavinia felt as if she was awake and ready for some new adventure. It was spring after all. Perhaps there was the possibility of a carriage ride to town or a trip to somewhere new? Mayhap they could visit Leeds in West Yorkshire or even York? Her thoughts of where she would like to go and what she wanted to see, were endless, as she made her way down the corridor, past the oil painting of her father, and down the stairs. The one person she did not to trouble herself thinking about, was Mr Keeling. She came to understand that he had left Yorkshire but did not hear where he went and never made any effort to learn about his whereabouts. It had been months since she had seen him or spoken to him – perhaps the spectre of Mr Keeling was gone from her life forever?

She entered the drawing room and was greeted by her grand-mother, who smiled her approval at Lavinia's choice of dress. "That colour suits you my dear. It does not call attention to you in the garish kind of way that some young women favour. I like the new style, with the fuller skirt – it is sensible and suitable for the occasion."

"What occasion is that?" Lavinia asked as she sat down on a couch beside Charlotte.

"You know full well that the vicar pays a call to Claxton Hall nearly every week, for tea, as his health permits. Today there may be a surprise in store for us, unless I have been deceived. I heard news from Mrs Eversley, whom I saw yesterday while I was in town," Mrs Talridge explained.

"Mrs Talridge, you tease Lavinia. Please tell her and put her mind at ease," Charlotte implored the older woman.

"I shall do no such thing. It has been a long time since we have had any cause for merriment in this house, and I will not be convinced to give away my secret, not for all the money in the county."

"Grandmother you already possess a generous amount of the money," Lavinia teased.

"Lavinia, it is not proper for a young lady to discuss financial matters, even jovially. Have I not taught you better than that?" Mrs Talridge said in mock indignation.

"Very well, I will not say another word about it, but Charlotte is quite right – it is terrible how you hold me in suspense, after all that I have been through," Lavinia said with a frown.

"Humph! The young have remarkable restorative powers, and I will not be fooled into believing that you still grieve for Mr Keeling. I have observed you smile once too often for a woman who is grieving for an inconstant suitor."

"Inconstant? Grandmother, he disappeared and abandoned me. Does that not garner your sympathy, even now?" Lavinia said with a mischievous glance towards Charlotte.

"Perhaps, my dear child, were it not for the talk you and I had when you fell ill a few days before your wedding, I would garner more sympathy," she said with a mischievous look in her eyes, "...but let us not talk about the past. This surprise is simply too wonderful to be ruined by anything as dull as telling you in mere words. If you would be patient, our vicar will be arriving soon, and then we may have tea. You shall know of this surprise soon enough."

Lavinia was intrigued by both her grandmother's wit and the surprise that awaited her. She had always respected and adored the vicar of Cotes Cross. He was a good man, a truly generous sort of person who cared deeply for the poor and the sick amongst the villagers, and Lavinia herself had been the recipient of his generosity when she was young. She enjoyed his visits to Claxton Hall nearly as much as she enjoyed working side by side with him and his wife, caring for the villagers in need. However, she sighed, that was before she had been confined to the house during her grandmother's imposed exile. She knew that she would find the vicar's visit to be engaging, but she could not imagine how she might contain her impatience to learn of this surprise, throughout his visit.

"Since it is now spring, perhaps I may be allowed to venture out more often? A trip into York or Leeds may be planned, with your permission, Grandmother," Lavinia asked, hopeful that Charlotte's presence and her grandmother's happy mood would be enough to convince Mrs Talridge to allow her to come and go as she pleased once again and to engage in society.

"We shall discuss that after the vicar's visit," Mrs Talridge said as the footman announced the arrival of their guest and of someone else whom Lavinia was not expecting.

"Mr James Harding and Mr Edward Fletcher," the footman said as he stood in the doorway.

The kind, older man was still able to walk with his hunched back and his cane – a miracle in her youthful eyes – and his features were as weathered as ever. Lavinia did not recognise the name of the second man, nor did she recognise his face as he entered the drawing room beside the vicar. The vicar's youthful companion was, however, as opposite as if they had been designed to contrast each other. The young man was as vigorous and straight in his posture as Father Harding, the parish vicar, was hunched. He was handsome, and he smiled in an unassuming way, which immediately put Lavinia at ease. His hair was as light in colour as Charlotte's blonde curls, his eyes were a bright blue, and his smile was as pleasant to look upon as his slender but not gaunt frame. He was a striking figure, dressed in the sombre black of his vicar's garb, but he wore the colour well.

Lavinia looked at Charlotte, stealing a moment with her companion as each lady raised their eyebrows in approval of this new acquaintance. Father Harding introduced the younger gentleman with an air of pride and satisfaction in his voice. After all the formalities had been observed, Mrs Talridge invited the men to be seated, as the footman brought in the tea service.

"Mr Fletcher, is it true that you shall be assisting Father Harding in his duties in the parish?" Mrs Talridge asked, as she smiled warmly at the young man.

"I shall be his assistant, but only in rudimentary tasks," Mr Fletcher explained, as he looked at his elderly companion with gentle, caring eyes.

Father Harding cleared his throat as he said, "My young assistant is not being entirely honest, as he is too modest to tell you the full extent of his responsibilities. He will be taking my place as vicar one day. I regret that I must retire... my memory and my health have left much to be desired lately. I was ill this winter, and I fear it may have sapped the last of my strength."

"Vicar, I'm very sorry to hear that, but where shall you go? Will you remain in Cotes Cross?" Lavinia asked, her concern for the vicar overwhelming her curiosity about Mr Fletcher.

"I shall take a house in the village for myself and my wife, although she insists that we journey to Bath to take the waters. I expect Mr Fletcher, here, will do a fine job and he will be welcomed by the families of the parish," the vicar said as he eyed the sandwiches and desserts displayed on fine china on the table. "Is that berry tart? How I love tarts."

The vicar amused himself, enjoying the berry tarts with his tea, as Lavinia stole glances at Mr Fletcher. Under her observation, she noted that he was attentive to Father Harding, not letting the older man want for anything, from a fresh napkin in his lap (when he dropped his), or a second serving of tarts. When Mr Fletcher caught her looking at him, he smiled as she blushed and turned away.

"Mr Fletcher, you haven't told us a single thing about yourself? Where are you from – do you hail from Yorkshire?" asked Mrs Talridge.

Mr Fletcher replied, "I wish that I were from Yorkshire. I find the countryside to be serene, and it offers a tranquil respite, but I do not claim to be from this county. I am from Manchester."

"Manchester? How will you adapt to such a change? Surely you must find Cotes Cross to be dull in comparison to a city?"

"I do not intend to disagree with you, Mrs Talridge, as you know the ways and the customs of this county far better than I, having just arrived. What I will say, is that I doubt I shall ever use the word 'dull' to describe Cotes Cross or this parish. There are many in need here, as Father Harding had told me before I agreed to the position, and it was for precisely that reason that I accepted the job, for I feel compelled to endeavour to do all I can to help others. Here in the village and the parish, there is much to be done to bring comfort to those without food and without hope, so I doubt I shall ever find the work here dull or dissatisfying."

"Mr Fletcher, if I may... I want to understand you correctly. Do you intend to work amongst the impoverished and the infirm?" Lavinia asked, finding the courage to speak to the handsome, young gentleman.

"I do, Miss Talridge," Mr Fletcher answered with a nod. "I do intend to do the Lord's work here. I feel that I am needed here, and that one person can change the fortunes of another in a place like Cotes Cross."

Lavinia was not quite sure she was hearing this man's words correctly or whether she was imagining them. Was he really saying what her heart had longed to hear from a gentleman of education and worth? That he cared for the poor, for the villagers, and that he was going to do his duty by them?

"Mr Fletcher, is it not the responsibility of the vicar to see to the needs of his parish?" Mrs Talridge asked with a gleam in her eye.

"It is the duty of the clergy, but it is also the duty of every man and woman who is able, and who has the means and the strength to do not only what is required, but whatever other good deeds they may find to do. Every person of conscience should do what they are able, to ensure the comfort and care of the lowest and poorest amongst us," the young man answered.

"You will find, Mrs Talridge, that Mr Fletcher is a capable and devoted member of the clergy. I believe he will be a welcome addition to our society," Father Harding said, with a smile directed at his companion.

"A welcome addition indeed," Mrs Talridge answered, as her gaze met Lavinia's.

Lavinia noticed that Charlotte had been particularly quiet, not saying very much, as she herself had said little. Mrs Talridge was in command of the drawing room, as she asked the questions of Mr Fletcher, that Lavinia wished to know the answers to and, she was certain, so did Charlotte. A flurry of shared looks and silent glances told Lavinia that she was not the only lady to appreciate the polite conversation and unassuming manners of their handsome guest.

Lavinia was also not the only person to notice the unusual lack of conversation, as Father Harding teased them benevolently, "My word, what has happened to you Miss Fenwick and Miss Talridge? I do not recall a tea where you have not peppered me with questions about the parish?"

Lavinia looked down at the tea cup in her hand – the level of the tea had hardly diminished, as she tried to think of an answer. Charlotte was slightly bolder, "We have not been quiet, only attentive to you and your new assistant."

"Attentive?" the old vicar chuckled, and Lavinia felt embarrassed. Had she and Charlotte both been transfixed by Mr Fletcher? Had they been obviously staring, in a manner that was indecent?

"Mr Fletcher, tell us about Manchester. I have never been to a city of that size. Are there very many people? What do the shops sell, and what do people eat in a place such as that?" Lavinia asked, feeling the necessity to engage in conversation, when all she wished was to ask more than was polite.

Listening to Mr Fletcher describe the city, she wondered whether he was engaged or married, and surprised herself with her own curiosity. There was no mention of a wife, so perhaps he was not married at all? Yet, a gentleman in possession of his countenance and pleasing manner, as well as his reputable position as a clergyman, could surely not be unattached, could he? She had never met a gentleman who was as pleasant and charming, but yet as unassuming as she found him to be. He did not frown, nor look at her as if he were appraising her, but more importantly his eyes sparkled as he laughed.

The visit was over entirely too soon for Lavinia as the vicar reached for his cane, signalling that the conversation had come to an end.

Mrs Talridge invited him, his wife, and his new assistant, Mr Fletcher, to return to Claxton Hall during the upcoming week, perhaps for dinner? She promised an invitation would be forthcoming, as Father Harding replied that he would be delighted. Lavinia wondered if Mr Fletcher would also be delighted to return, as she bid him a good day.

Mrs Applegate and her daughter, Jane, arrived just as the vicar and Mr Fletcher were leaving; an inconvenience that while slightly inopportune, Lavinia accepted with grace. She wished to speak with Charlotte and her grandmother in private regarding the new clergyman, and she was not disappointed. Jane and her mother seemed to want to discuss the exact same subject, as soon as the gentlemen were away.

"Mrs Applegate, Miss Applegate won't you have tea? I can have a fresh pot and tarts brought from the kitchen," Mrs Talridge said as she invited the women to be seated.

"Thank you no, there is no need to trouble yourself," Mrs Applegate said, eyeing the empty plate where the tarts had been, now desolate with only crumbs in the place of the sweets.

Mrs Talridge acted as if she had not heard her guests. Despite their polite refusal, she summoned the footman to arrange for a fresh pot of tea and more tarts to be brought at once. As Mrs Talridge was occupied and as Mrs Applegate reiterated that there was no need to bother, Jane Applegate, who was seated in a chair next to Lavinia's side of the couch, leaned over and whispered to her friend about the new clergyman.

"Was that Mr Fletcher at tea? Oh, he is dashing, isn't he?" Jane said to Lavinia.

"I suppose he is, but what if he is attached? Wouldn't it be terribly wrong to be discussing him in those terms, if he is promised to someone?" Lavinia asked.

"Wrong? I doubt we are doing anything wrong by admiring him." Jane replied.

"Lavinia, what are you and Miss Applegate discussing in whispers? It is impolite to whisper in the drawing room at tea," Mrs Talridge, offered her opinion.

"We weren't whispering, we simply did not want to interrupt your discussion with Mrs Applegate," explained Lavinia.

"And what, pray tell, were you and Miss Applegate *not* whispering about?" Mrs Talridge asked, as she peered at the young ladies.

"I was asking your granddaughter if that was Mr Fletcher I saw in the hall a moment ago," Jane answered.

With a bored air, Mrs Talridge answered the question, "Yes, it was Mr Fletcher."

"Mr Fletcher at Claxton Hall? I dare say you have received him before many of the other families in the county," Mrs Applegate stated.

"We are fortunate that the vicar holds us in such high regard," Mrs Talridge explained, "I was impressed by the young man and very impressed by his manners... he had a good Christian look to him. I believe he will do well in Cotes Cross, although I shall not be at all pleased to see Father Harding retired."

"I heard that Mr Fletcher is the son of a baronet," Jane said, as the footman returned to the drawing room with a tray containing a pot of tea and more tarts.

"A baronet? I heard he is the son of man who made his fortune from the mines in Cornwall," Mrs Applegate suggested.

"Is he engaged?" Charlotte asked.

"Or married?" Lavinia added.

"If he were engaged or married, I believe that Father Harding would have told us at once," Mrs Talridge declared. "It is my belief that he is neither engaged nor attached. What gentleman accepts a position in a village such as Cotes Cross, if he has any hope of raising a family?"

"What of our own dear Father Harding? *He* is married," Lavinia replied.

"He is married, but he also inherited a modest annuity, and does not rely solely on his income as vicar. However, we should not discuss his business affairs, Lavinia," her grandmother rebuked.

"Perhaps the same could be said for Mr Fletcher? If he is the son of a baronet or his father owns mines, he must have a generous income of his own," Jane said, as she filled a plate with tarts.

Lavinia wondered whether Mr Fletcher was a man of wealth and rank, and if he was indeed unattached, as her grandmother had suggested. She wondered a lot of things about Mr Fletcher, but she knew that she wouldn't discover the answers to any of her questions, sitting at tea.

Chapter 13

As the warm months of spring surrendered to the heat of summer, Lavinia often found herself in the company of Mr Fletcher, as if her grandmother were purposely engineering that outcome. Mr Fletcher was invited to tea, in the company of the vicar. He was a frequent guest at informal dinners, and Mrs Talridge insisted that she, Charlotte, and Lavinia visit the parsonage with increasingly regularity. Lavinia did not mind the visits to Cotes Cross, in fact, in a lot of ways, she still considered the village home. Those visits also afforded her with opportunities to see the vicar and his new assistant, in which visits she found herself drawn to Mr Fletcher for more than his handsome face and his charm. His kindness gave her a reason to seek out his company, and she discovered that he was as impassioned by the same cause that she so fervently believed in.

The visits to the parsonage increased as the summer wore on, until Charlotte Fenwick was called away from Yorkshire by a happy but urgent letter from her sister. Her eldest sister had been married for many years to a clerk, who worked in a modest but respectable solicitors' firm in Chester, in the county of Cheshire. It was an unexpected letter, which was thrilling to Charlotte, as she told Lavinia. After many childless years, her sister was due to have her first child and wanted Charlotte to be with her during the last weeks of her confinement. Having been a loyal governess and companion, Charlotte was permitted to take as much time as was required. Mrs Talridge sent her to stay with her sister, carrying a hamper of broth and freshly baked bread. There was also money in her pocket for traveling expenses.

Without Charlotte as her companion, Lavinia and her grandmother were left on their own – a state which Mrs Talridge was quick to exploit.

On the morning following Charlotte's happy but apprehensive departure, Mrs Talridge instructed the footmen to have the carriage brought round. After breakfast, she and her granddaughter made their way to Cotes Cross, to the parsonage.

It was a beautiful summer morning and the dew clung to the grass as a soft haze lay close to the moors. At the church house, the garden was in full bloom under the shade of the enormous trees in the churchyard. Mrs Talridge was welcomed by the vicar and his wife, as Lavinia sought the company of Mr Fletcher, who she understood was attending to chores in the parsonage garden.

Lifting her skirts as high as she dared, she tried to keep her dress dry as her shoes were soaked through from the dew. She did not mind the cool feeling of having wet feet. She longed to slip off her shoes and stockings and run wild, but she knew that as a proper young lady, that behaviour was entirely out of the question. She would not dare to do such a thing in front of Mr Fletcher or anyone else, not even Charlotte. Careful not to expose an ankle, she sought the stone path, as she searched for Mr Fletcher.

The morning light filtered through tree limbs overhead, and she saw the familiar profile of the young man. He was on his knees weeding a row of carrots and was wearing a waistcoat and a shirt that was rolled up to his elbows, as he worked, unaware of her observation. She did not know if she should interrupt him, as he seemed to be consumed by the task at hand. How handsome he looked, even as he was weeding a garden! It was a task she could not imagine a man of rank doing, as long as there were servants and staff to do the work for him. If it was true that Mr Fletcher was the son of a wealthy mine owner or a baronet, it was remarkable that he should choose a life of charity and good work, instead of serving in a city where he might seek promotion and patronage in a large parish.

Lavinia's contemplation was soon put to an abrupt, but not unhappy end, when Mr Fletcher shifted his position and realised he was not alone. Dropping his spade into the basket with the weeds, he got to his feet, unrolled his shirt sleeves and greeted her, "Miss Talridge, what brings you to the parsonage so early in the morning? I trust it isn't bad luck or illness?"

"Nothing of the sort. My grandmother and I are in good health."

"What of Miss Fenwick? I do not see her with you. Is she well?"

"She is well. I have not heard otherwise, as she left to pay a visit to her family yesterday."

"That is good news indeed. Health is something for which we should be thankful, when so many others do not have the blessing of health or strength," he said as he reached for his jacket, which was lying haphazardly on a wooden bench. "I offer you my sincerest apologies that you have found me in this disgraceful state of undress. If I had known that I would be receiving company, I should have dressed with care and not allowed myself to appear so slovenly. Forgive me."

"Mr Fletcher, there is nothing to forgive. It is I who surprised you with my sudden appearance. There is no wrongdoing on your part, if you are not dressed for my intrusion into the sanctuary of your garden. As to the suggestion that you are slovenly... I cannot see how that can be true. You take care in your appearance and your manner of dress," she said, and as she did so, she realised that by saying so, she was admitting that she had noticed him and noticed his appearance.

"Thank you for the compliment," he said as he adjusted the collar of his jacket, "It delights me that you do not consider me to be less than fastidious in my grooming or my choice of attire."

Lavinia felt the heat rising to her cheeks as she blushed. Looking away, she tried to conceal her embarrassment by changing the subject to anything other than his appearance (which she did find more than pleasing). "Your garden seems to be a success. Have you always tended your own gardens and grown your own vegetables?"

"I have a confession to make. I have not always grown my own vegetables, or much else. The vicar has shared his knowledge of gardening with me, which I find to be a task that is as humbling as it is necessary. Growing food for the vicar and his wife, and for the use of anyone who is in need, is satisfying."

"Mr Fletcher, I hope you do not mind my impertinence, but I am astounded that you, an educated man of the church, would stoop to as menial a task as gardening."

Mr Fletcher smiled.

"I believe it is because I am a man of the church, that I find the task so appealing. It teaches me humility, as I am forced to weed the carrots again and again, never truly gaining victory over my foe, the weeds."

Lavinia giggled, "Your foe, the weeds?"

"I admit it is not as elegant a foe as the Norman invaders or the Picts but there you are. My foe is sin, poverty, and these weeds," he laughed as he gestured to the basket filled with dead plants.

"How you talk, Mr Fletcher! You are unlike any gentleman I have ever known."

"I hope that was meant as a compliment," he said, and his blue eyes glistened in the soft sunlight of morning.

"If you knew the gentlemen in my acquaintance, you would understand that, yes, I did speak out of turn. I wished to compliment you, and I hope you do not take what I said as anything other than I intended."

"Of course not, Miss Talridge. We shall not speak of it anymore. Shall I escort you to the parsonage, where you might find tea waiting?"

"That would be lovely, but tea was not the reason for the visit."

"What was the reason?" he asked, his blue eyes peering into hers.

"Charlotte and I have been working on clothing for the young children of the farm workers. Grandmother and I thought that Father Harding and you may be able to distribute them, as they are undoubtedly needed."

"You sewed the clothes yourselves? You and Miss Fenwick?"

"Yes, I have some talent with the needle, although I find embroidery to be easier than plain work."

"It is very generous of you to spend your time in such a pursuit. Not many women in your station would lower themselves to sewing clothes for the infants and children of farm help."

"I do not think myself above these people or their society. I wish to see them live in dignity and comfort. If I can do anything for them, it is my dearest wish."

"I think I understand your interest in the villagers of Cotes Cross, as the vicar did speak to me of your rather unusual history."

Lavinia was startled but did not show. Lavinia did not think that Father Harding knew that her mother was unwed. Were her hopes concerning Mr Fletcher to be dashed before they began, if he thought of her as unworthy of his attention?

"About my history, I wish the vicar hadn't mentioned that to you."

"There is no shame in being poor, Miss Talridge. What he said seems to be confirmed by your interest in the village and your talent for sewing."

"Oh?" Lavinia asked, curious about what Mr Fletcher knew. "What did he say, if I may ask?"

"You have to assure me that you shall not be upset with him, after all, he is growing older and his health is a bother to him... He was confiding in me what he thought I should know in order to administer to the spiritual needs of the parish. You would not find the least fault in what he said, regarding your mother, as he gave her praise for her skill. He admired you, for your tenacity and your continued devotion to the people you knew as a child. He told me that you were raised here in the village, but that you were left an orphan, and he told me that you and your mother were well-respected here in Cotes Cross, as is your grandmother."

"Is that all, or was there anything else?" Lavinia asked silently.

"Yes, there was... but I hesitate to discuss it, as it may cause you embarrassment," Mr Fletcher said as they drew near the parsonage.

"If it is about my mother..." she said hesitating to finish the sentence.

"No, it was about your unfortunate luck last year, but I do not want to mention a subject that is none of my affair."

"You mean my wedding to Mr Keeling? There is nothing embarrassing about that, except to my pride which is not much wounded by the incident, if that was all he said." Lavinia replied calmly.

"I assure you, you have my word Miss Talridge, it was all the vicar said. Forgive me for bringing the matter up, as I meant to tell you that I understand your interest in the people of the village, and it does you credit. Not many young ladies who have risen in the ranks of wealth and property would trouble themselves with the commoners they once knew as their equals, and I am impressed by your generosity."

Lavinia considered what he had said as they walked into the parsonage. He was impressed by her generosity and he did not seem to be bothered in the least by her past. She wondered if he would feel as impressed if he knew the truth behind her birth, but she chose not to dwell on that unfortunate business, at that moment.

There was much to be discussed that morning. Mr Fletcher had a great number of ideas for improving the village school, for providing medical care to the villagers, and for seeing to the care of those families who were in danger of starvation. Lavinia felt that the village of Cotes Cross would be lucky to have such a man as their new vicar, after the beloved Father Harding retired.

Mr Fletcher was ideal in so many ways, that she did not mind his impertinence at asking her about her past; a past she had not shared with Mr Keeling. Perhaps that was the difference between the men – Mr Keeling had a way of making her feel as if she and all who did not share his rank were not worthy of his notice, while Mr Fletcher was the opposite. He treated all manner of men with respect and did not seem to regard her former status, as a humble orphan, to be of any consequence. Oh, how delightful Mr Fletcher was! She wished for a man just like him for her husband.

She knew that Cotes Cross had found its champion, and she had found the kind of man she could respect, and perhaps he was the kind of man she could love.

Chapter 14

Autumn came to Yorkshire in cold chilly mornings and days that grew shorter. It was nearly two years since Mr Keeling had abandoned Lavinia and Yorkshire. For two years, Lavinia had devoted herself to the people she knew and loved. There were barely any outbreaks of illness or any other deprivation that occurred, without Lavinia and Reverend Fletcher working tirelessly to see that those who suffered were cared for. She was too devoted to her work to notice, except on rare occasions, that she was still not wed. She supposed it was because she was working beside the one man she wished would show her the slightest indication that he considered her to be more than merely a generous benefactress to the village, or a caring patroness of the downtrodden.

How many times had she been alone with Reverend Fletcher – not in an improper way, but as they walked through the village or worked in each other's company? He, like Charlotte, had become a friend and a companion, but that was all. He showed not the slightest interest in her, for any other reason than she was a young woman of means who devoted her time to charity. Lavinia nursed her hopes and dreams of a match with Reverend Fletcher, and she was content to be his companion, but still she found a way to keep her hopes alive, as he had not discussed marriage with her or anyone else. This was strange to Lavinia, considering that he was the vicar of the parish, and had been for nearly a year, ever since Father Harding's retirement.

Lavinia suspected that Charlotte was the one person in the world who may have suspected that she was somewhat in love with Reverend Fletcher. At one point, in the autumn after Reverend Fletcher had arrived in Cotes Cross, Lavinia thought that Charlotte may have harboured feelings for the gentleman, but she soon realised that Reverend Fletcher had not expressed feelings for anyone in the village or the county, well, at least as far as Lavinia knew. He seemed to be as devoted to his work as she was to her charity. Perhaps, she sometimes thought to herself, when she was alone, there was a possibility, however remote, that he cared for Lavinia as much as she cared for him. She dwelled on that chance, that slim hope, far surpassing even her grandmother's hopes that she would become the vicar's wife.

On a cold afternoon, late in the season, Lavinia was sitting beside the fireside while Charlotte read aloud from a novel. Mrs Talridge was in the study as rain fell heavily outside. Lavinia was not expecting any visitors that day, because the weather was so inhospitable. The roads would surely be muddy, and the rivers would be raging torrents of flood waters. It had rained for three days without end and, privately, Lavinia worried about the villagers and how they were faring.

She did not know that this was to be the day her fortunes were to change forever.

Change in life can come in many forms. It can come with illness or with accident, as Lavinia well knew. This alteration to her fortunes came in the form of a letter, but the letter was not brought to Claxton Hall by a footman or by a man sent to convey the urgency and importance of the missive – instead it came quietly disguised as normal correspondence from Mrs Talridge's solicitor in London. Mrs Talridge opened the letter as absentmindedly as she did with all correspondence from her solicitor. She had no suit pressing, having settled favourably with the viscount two years ago. Glancing at the letter as she sipped her tea, she nearly choked on the hot drink as she read what was written on the page.

The news in the letter was dramatic enough to make her forget all of the business that awaited her attention that day. Setting the cup of tea down on her desk, to avoid dropping it, she read the letter and then sat back in the chair, staring at the room and all its furnishings as if she had never really seen them until now. For years, since the death of her husband and her son, she had had the use of Claxton Hall. It was hers for her lifetime and then it was to be inherited by her nephew. The rooms of the great house and its fine furnishings were, at least in her mind, on loan to her until that moment when her nephew (whom she had not seen for a decade) would take possession of the house and everything else that belonged to her.

After recovering somewhat from the shock of the letter, she slowly walked from the study to the drawing room. She stopped outside the door before entering and listened, as she thought of what she should say to her granddaughter. Charlotte's melodious voice echoed in the cavernous room as she read from a novel. Lavinia's bright, clear laugh rang out from time to time, as the two women enjoyed their time together, without the intrusion of guests. Steeling herself for their shocked reactions, Mrs Talridge pulled herself up to her tallest height and, holding her head up high, she walked into the room like the mistress of the house that she was and always would be.

"Mrs Talridge," Charlotte said in her cheerful manner as she closed the pages of the book, marking her place with a pretty piece of ribbon.

"Charlotte, Lavinia," Mrs Talridge said as she closed the door behind herself, before she strode across the room towards the warmth of the fireplace.

"I was not expecting to see you until dinner," Lavinia said as her grandmother passed directly in front of her, taking a place of prominence beside the mantle.

"Shall we ring for refreshments? It is early for tea, but the footman can be summoned if you wish," asked Charlotte.

"I am well aware that a footman can be summoned, thank you," Mrs Talridge said with more force and venom than she wished. Seeing Charlotte's hurt expression, the older woman immediately felt regret. "I did not intend to say that to you, in that manner. I have just received news of a most pressing nature that cannot wait."

Charlotte seemed to forget the slight against her as quickly as it had occurred. "Why don't you sit down? You look pale."

"Do I? That is of no consequence."

"Grandmother, what is this news?" Lavinia instantly thought of Father Harding; he was in Bath with his wife. His health was failing, and she suspected that she would hear bad news at any time regarding this beloved man, who had been so kind to her all these years.

"It is terrible... It has caused me no end of distress, yet it may not be distressing to you, my dear Lavinia. When you hear what I have to tell you, your life shall be forever altered. Even more so, I dare say, than when I found you in that small hovel as a child."

"Grandmother?" Lavinia reached for Charlotte.

"If you are prepared my dear, I shall tell you. As there is no need to hide the circumstances, Charlotte, you may stay."

Charlotte held Lavinia's hand in her own, and the two younger women stared at Mrs Talridge who stood as a statue at the mantle. The tension and gravity of the situation weighed heavily upon her shoulders.

"Lavinia, you recall that Claxton Hall and all its contents – the estate, the property and holdings – were to be deeded to my nephew?"

"Yes," Lavinia said as she stared at her grandmother, wide-eyed and apprehensive.

"Your dowry and annuity are modest but settled to be had no matter what fortune could bring to my estate or the holdings of the Talridge family. Do you recall that arrangement?" Mrs Talridge asked.

"I do." Lavinia's face turned nearly as pale as the ash in the grate of the fireplace.

"My dear, something has happened that will greatly affect your dowry, your annuity, and the entire estate."

"Tell me Grandmother. I promise to bear it. I am not a stranger to poverty. I can live by my wits if I must," Lavinia tried to say with a determined look in her eyes.

"That will not be necessary. Your fortune *has* changed but not in the way that you believe. My nephew, the heir to Claxton Hall and all that I possess, has been reported missing. He has been missing for many months, but as it occurred in the West Indies, the news did not reach my solicitor until a very short time ago. My nephew is presumed to have perished. The solicitor advised me that unless my nephew is found alive in the following two weeks, he shall be declared dead."

Lavinia stared at her grandmother, as she held tightly to Charlotte's hand. She did not say a word as Charlotte whispered to her,

"Lavinia, say something."

"She does not have to say anything in response. How can she? She has just discovered that she is the sole heiress to all that I own, my estate, my house... everything. Her life has changed and so has yours, dear Charlotte. You are the companion of one of the wealthiest young women in Yorkshire and the whole of the North of England."

Lavinia looked from Charlotte's face to her grandmother's as she said, "I am sorry for your loss. I do not remember my cousin, but this must be terrible for you Grandmother. What is to be done?"

"His loss is sorely felt, but not as keenly as you might expect. He has been gone for all of these many years, we were never close, and the reason he stood to inherit my property is not important any more. You, my dear, do not have to do anything at all. I, however, have much that needs to be done. We must be away to London... there are accounts to be settled and paperwork that must be drawn up at once... but that is not all."

"It is not?" Lavinia asked as if she were in a daze.

"No Lavinia," her grandmother replied. "You are an heiress, but you are twenty. You are still young enough to do well in your first season, but you shall have to move quickly, so you are not overlooked in favour of the younger women with better connections. We have no time to waste! The season will be beginning soon, and you shall have the finest dresses, the most stylish bonnets and all that you require in order to find a husband worthy of your new station in life. Once you have recovered, make arrangements to pack your clothes, your books, and whatever else you wish to bring. I will notify my staff to have the house in London prepared. We leave at once!"

Chapter 15

After a quiet life of solitary pursuits and evenings spent with a good book and the companionship of her grandmother and Charlotte, Lavinia was not prepared for London. She had visited London once or twice in her youth, in the company of her grandmother, but never during the season. As she recalled, the visits were always over quickly, as her grandmother did not want to expose Lavinia to the dissolute temptations of city life. Mrs Talridge adored London, with its fashion and its sights, but she cared more for Lavinia. She insisted on a traditional country upbringing, which she thought would benefit a young woman who showed no particular inclination towards drawing, music, or any of the other accomplishments which might require the engagement of tutors or exposure to London.

Lavinia also suspected that her grandmother's insistence that they not join the other wealthy families in London may have been her fault. How would she have fared in London competing against the daughters of dukes and wealthy landowners? Although her grandmother had never said it, Lavinia knew implicitly that she had a far better chance of marriage in Yorkshire, where there were fewer women of worth. Forthwith, her unfortunate birth, her lack of connections, and her unconventional youth could all be overlooked now that she was wealthy or would be wealthy one day.

Lavinia was not sure what to make of the change in her fortune. Although it was March, and the height of the season, she was still unaccustomed to the world of London society. Her grandmother spoke often, in private, of her abandonment by Mr Keeling and pronounced that he had been a fool. If Mr Keeling had not left Lavinia on her wedding day, he would have stood to inherit the vast Talridge fortune; a fortune, Mrs Talridge boasted, that might be in excess of the Viscount of Wharton's, since she had also inherited her nephew's property, upon his death. Her nephew had died childless and unmarried in the West Indies. Mrs Talridge, and by extension Lavinia, would inherit every penny of her cousin's money, making her even richer than Mrs Talridge could describe.

All of this fortune, which included merchant ships, tea plantations, cattle and sheep farms, and great swathes of property, left Lavinia's head spinning. She had somehow risen from 'daughter of a sewing woman, living in a hovel', to a woman worth more than most of the celebrated heiresses in London. This fact was not lost on the Ton, a select clique of well-to-do aristocrats who served as the unofficial guardians of London's high society. Charlotte explained that these people, this inner circle, were devilishly tricky and unforgiving. They also held the keys to the upper echelons of the upper class. Even if Lavinia was wealthy and even if she had been born the daughter of a count, they might still deny her entrance to the best parties and refuse to invite her to their homes for dinner – in other words, generally shut her out of the top tiers of society. They could easily leave her, like so many other hopefuls, to squander her time amongst the knights and second sons, the penniless and the titled, or the wealthy merchant classes.

Unknown to Lavinia, her grandmother was well-received by the Ton, even if she was not a more active member of society who was coming to London during the season. It was Mrs Talridge who insisted that Lavinia brush up on her skills in music, in order to impress Lady Cavendish and Lady Whitfield, two of the Ton's more selective members. If Lavinia was accepted by these ladies well then, her grandmother assured her, she would be received into any home in London. Her past would be well forgotten (or at least not investigated). She assured Lavinia that she would be able to choose a husband from amongst the wealthiest of men.

Lavinia wondered how she would suddenly become adept at playing music when she had not practiced in years, and she wondered if these women, or anyone else in society, would have the slightest interest in her if she were to tell them that she grew up in a village smaller than most of the parks in London. All of this business with being accepted or permitted to be part of the Ton seemed ridiculous when she thought about the poor beggars who she saw on the streets of London, or the suffering of the men who had returned from the war, missing limbs or unable to see. How could she put her effort towards anything as frivolous as gaining the acceptance of a group of wealthy, snobbish women?

She stared out the window of the vast house, which was not only located in a fashionable neighbourhood, but which stood like a sentinel to the park. Its grey, stone façade rose three storeys above the street, and it had one storey below street level, which contained the kitchen. Corinthian stone columns supported the roof of an entrance that was as imposing as the house had seemed to Lavinia the first time she had seen it as a young girl. Inside was just as impressive; the marble floors, the gleaming trim, the hand-painted murals, and the damask wall coverings in the rooms. Lavinia watched carriages bustling by and birds flying from tree to tree, along the street. It was the afternoon. Soon, it would be the busy hour in the park for carriage rides and promenades and here she sat at the piano of the music room, in a grand house overlooking Hyde Park. Taking carriage rides in the open air was one of her favourite pastimes, even if it was cold. She also enjoyed promenades with Charlotte at her side, as they walked along the wide pathways of the park, observing the fashions of the ladies who passed them, and while Lavinia and Charlotte noticed that they were often the subject of envy as they wore the latest styles, made of the finest material, not a single day had passed in which Lavinia had forgotten where she had come from.

Lavinia looked at the sheet music in front of her. The notes floated on the page, one looking like the next, until she could stand it no longer. She did not care one whit about Lady Cavendish or Lady Whitfield. If they wanted to hear music being played, they were welcome to engage a pianist.

Lavinia felt the need to go outside and as she was leaving the music room, she looked for Charlotte. Lavinia's grandmother would be gone to the shops on Bond Street for an hour or two, which left Lavinia time for a promenade with Charlotte. Finding her companion in the sunny sitting room on the second floor, Lavinia rushed to her side. "Charlotte, if we hurry, we can be in the park for the busy hour, for promenade. Please come with me... You know I am not permitted to go alone... remember how grandmother scolded me about going out by myself in London?"

"Lavinia, you're supposed to be practicing your music."

"I know I am, but I cannot play another note. If you come with me, we shall go for a short walk, and then I promise to practice."

"What of your grandmother? Has she given her permission? You know how upset she can be if you do not do as she wishes!"

"I know how she becomes, but the afternoon is warm today. It is pleasant for March, and we shall not be gone long... I cannot bear it any longer. I must have some air, or I shall perish. Please say that we can go?"

"We are not dressed properly."

"We shall wear our long pelisses. No-one will notice, I assure you."

"If you insist, who am I to say no? It is because of you that I am even in London."

"That does not matter, Charlotte, please be my friend and come with me," Lavinia said with a smile.

"I am your friend, but we will dress warmly. It will never do to be taken ill when we are to attend the ball at the Sutherlands tomorrow evening."

Lavinia agreed to dress as Charlotte suggested and fifteen minutes later, she met Charlotte at the front door of the house. She knew all too well that the footmen and the maids would tell her Grandmother that she and Charlotte had left for an hour, but she did not care about that. She wanted to be out of the stuffy house as she could not bear another minute inside, not when the March sunshine beckoned to her.

Across the street, Lavinia saw the parade of horse-drawn carriages making their way slowly around the park. She watched fashionable upper-class ladies sitting in the open carriages as they passed, dressed in their finest dresses, trimmed in fur. She did not care about riding in a carriage this afternoon. Instead she longed to walk and do anything but be seated at the piano bench for what felt like hours.

"Oh look, doesn't that gentleman appear to be Reverend Fletcher?" asked Lavinia as she pointed in the direction of a man on a tall white horse who was riding in the park.

"You think every gentleman looks like Reverend Fletcher. Have you not received a letter from him? Is he foremost on your mind?" Charlotte asked Lavinia.

"I *have* received a letter, but it has been a week since it arrived. He wrote to me that he is coming to London in a month."

"Lavinia, how will you meet a suitable gentleman if you do nothing with your time but seek out Reverend Fletcher? You are an heiress; you can have your pick of all the gentlemen here in town."

"I may have my pick, but are any of the gentlemen as kind and caring as Reverend Fletcher? Do they have a compassionate nature or spend their hours tending to the poor and downtrodden? How can I be content with a gentleman who is blind to the suffering of all around him?"

Charlotte struggled to keep up with the pace set by Lavinia. Breathlessly, she answered, "I would never presume that you marry a gentleman who did not share your interest in philanthropy. If you marry a wealthy aristocrat, think of the good you may do. The poor of the district that you will call home shall benefit from your attentions and your husband's connections."

"You talk as though I am engaged. I have not met a single suitable man whom I would wish to marry," Lavinia replied.

"Are you certain of that? I have observed that you spent a considerable amount of time in the company of Reverend Fletcher. When you were at Claxton Hall, you were never far from the gentleman."

"I do not deny that I am often in the company of Reverend Fletcher, but it is to no avail. He regards me as a generous patroness of the village of Cotes Cross and nothing more."

"You share a correspondence, and that may be some indication that he considers you to be more than *just* a benefactress of the villagers. I presumed that an understanding existed, in order for you to allow a correspondence."

"There is no understanding. He has never spoken of any regard or feeling for me other than the camaraderie of working to aid those who need help in the village," Lavinia confessed, although she did not like to admit the truth.

She longed for the young vicar to express some feeling for her other than polite regard, and appreciation for her assistance. He was always kind, and he had never made her feel as if she was beneath his notice, but yet, he did not speak to her as anything other than a close acquaintance – simply as a vicar might speak to a member of his church whom he considered a friend. Sometimes Lavinia wished for more than a friendship with him, but she had yet to receive even the slightest indication that she might hope for a future at his side.

Charlotte appeared perplexed, "If there is no understanding between you, then why do you write to him? It is not proper for a woman of your rank to send letters to a gentleman... it would appear forward, if it became known."

"How could a simple letter or two exchanged with the vicar of the village appear to be forward? I assure you that is all it is, and nothing more. There can hardly be a scandal in my interest in the charitable work being conducted in the village, while I am away," Lavinia said quickly.

"In your position you must be careful that nothing more is known of it. It may be of little interest to anyone in Yorkshire, but here in London, the rules of society are observed with strictness."

Lavinia laughed, "How can you say they are observed at all? I have seen ladies behaving as flirts and gentlemen forgetting themselves after drinking too much wine."

"You may have seen married women behaving in a regrettable manner and wealthy titled lords doing as they pleased, but certainly *not* unmarried women seeking husbands. Your behaviour must *always* be above reproach. There cannot be the slightest hint of a rumour about you, if you seek entry to the Ton."

"I do not seek entry to a group of people who are as wasteful in their spending or as critical of others as they. It is my grandmother's wish that I be accepted into their society," Lavinia groaned, lamenting her present state. "If I had been consulted, I would have wished for an acquaintance with good people, of the sort we knew in Yorkshire and who I know are not concerned with my worth rather than my opinions."

"You must not allow your grandmother to hear you say such a thing – the shock would be calamitous for her!" Charlotte replied.

"It is the truth. How I long to be free of this endless cycle of dinners, balls, and social engagements. I want to go for long walks on Bond

Street, to take in the sights and the shops. I wish to spend more than a passing hour in the park. I want to seek out the good people of this fair city and offer my wealth and my time to help those less fortunate souls who have not the means to feed themselves nor their children. I know full well that I shall not be permitted to do as my heart desires, and to offer my assistance to a charitable institution. If I was a bold person, I would insist that we return to Yorkshire at once."

"Lavinia! You cannot tell your grandmother any of what you have shared with me. Do you not understand why we are here? We are not languishing in town for my benefit or your grandmother's, although I believe she enjoys the society... We are here so that you may find a husband."

"I do wonder if you may be unable to find a suitable husband when it is plain that you hold Reverend Fletcher in such high regard."

Groaning again, Lavinia replied, "I understand the necessity of our visit, but this place and these people, are not to my liking. It will be spring soon, in Yorkshire. The flowers will bloom, the fields will be green, and the moors will wake from their slumbers. How I wish I could be there to walk along the lanes and to avail myself of the simple pastoral pleasures of my home."

"Are you including Reverend Fletcher amongst those simple pastoral pleasures that you miss?"

"Charlotte, how shocking you are!" Lavinia smiled. "I cannot feign to deny it – yes, I would like very much to see him again. It has been months since we last spoke."

Despite the sunshine that bathed the park in a golden afternoon light, a chill still pervaded the air. It was warm but the breezes were quite cold. Lavinia was glad that she was wearing her pelisse over her afternoon dress, as she shivered while she was thinking about the correct answer to Charlotte's assertion that she compared all her potential suitors to Reverend Fletcher. She could not disagree with her companion's observation, but she wished it were not so. How trying it was to find a gentleman who was everything she wished for in a husband, but who was not interested in fulfilling the position.

Charlotte stopped with an abruptness that caught Lavinia off guard, as she was searching for an answer that would not include a confession.

Charlotte's features were frozen in a look of horror as she gripped Lavinia's arm.

"What is the matter?" Lavinia asked, feeling Charlotte's fingers digging into the fabric of her clothes.

"I do not wish to alarm you, but I fear you may be startled in very short order!"

"Startled… what in the heavens? Is it grandmother?"

"No, Lavinia, it is not your grandmother. It is an apparition, a ghost from your past, that I fear will cause you to become faint. Here, take my hand, if you must!" Charlotte released her grip on Lavinia's arm, to Lavinia's relief, as she offered her a gloved hand.

"Charlotte, what has –?"

"Look there, in the distance. Do you not see who has caused me such distress?" Charlotte asked, as she gestured to the approaching gentleman, riding a tall, dark steed.

It was difficult for Lavinia to describe exactly how she felt at that moment, but she was barely able to breathe. Ahead, on the path, was a man she knew far too well. She instantly recognised the tilt of his aristocratic head, his haughty bearing, and the imperious look on his face.

"How can it be?" Lavinia's voice sounded like a distant whisper to her own ears. "He disappeared... and I presumed he had run away to the east somewhere, to China perhaps, or the Indies? Is that truly Mr Keeling we are seeing?"

"Lavinia, I fear he has not disappeared. He is dressed in a red coat, and I believe he is wearing regimentals... He is surely seated upon that horse and he is heading towards us. Shall we make haste, shall we turn and leave?" Charlotte asked, as she held onto Lavinia's hand.

Lavinia recalled this man's ill treatment of her with perfect clarity, which had culminated in his abandonment of her on their wedding day.

"No, Charlotte, we shall not turn and run away like frightened rabbits. It is he who should be embarrassed to see us, and it is he who should be the one to change course. I say we continue with our stroll as though he matters not one whit."

"If you insist... although I have no hope of being convincingly duplicitous, if he should attempt to make amends," Charlotte replied.

"Neither do I. He may be of a higher rank and an officer, but he is no longer in possession of any more wealth that I shall possess one day. Let him come, and we shall act as if he were a stranger who has not been introduced."

Lavinia held her head up and dropped her friend's hand as she glared towards the rider who was fast approaching. There was no mistake; the man on the horse was Mr Keeling. She could see his features without any obfuscation, and it was undoubtedly the gentleman who may once have been her husband. As he drew closer, Lavinia felt her breath catch in the back of her throat – however, she refused to show any reaction to his sudden appearance.

A carriage slowed as the rider approached, and Lavinia breathed a sigh of relief. The lady inside the carriage and her companion were both well-dressed women. Lavinia could tell from their fur-lined pelisses and the style of bonnets, that they were in possession of sufficient income to afford such luxuries. Charlotte and Lavinia stepped out of the way as the carriage came to a halt and the rider, Mr Keeling, reigned in his horse. With a tilt of his hat, he greeted the women under Lavinia's watchful gaze, seemingly not having noticed Charlotte's or her nearby presence. She was relieved that the ladies had stolen Mr Keeling's attention, as she was not looking forward to an awkward moment when he passed her. She dreaded that she would be forced to acknowledge him or to ignore him as the scoundrel he was.

"Shall we return to the house? I did promise you I would practice my music, after our stroll?" Lavinia asked, as she turned away from the scene playing out in front of her.

"Yes, Lavinia, I believe the weather has taken a turn, and we should go back home," Charlotte replied quickly. "The fire will be as welcoming as I am sure a cup of tea will be, after our exertions."

As they were leaving, Lavinia could not help but turn her head once more to take a final look at Mr Keeling. He was smiling as he nodded to the women in the carriage and Lavinia heard him laugh, a deep melodious sound that was unexpected from a man she recalled as being perpetually stern. She was curious as to what could be the cause for his merriment, and she strained to listen. Lavinia could not overhear their voices, but she could tell from his reaction that what was being said was to Mr Keeling's liking.

For a fleeting moment she wondered whether he knew of her change of fortune. Would that have made the slightest difference when he chose to leave her on their wedding day?

Without warning, he suddenly looked away from the ladies and, to Lavinia's horror, stared directly at her.

She stood transfixed as their eyes locked across the distance.

It was Charlotte's gentle but insistent tug on her arm that pulled Lavinia's attention from the gaze of Mr Keeling. How dare he look at her after what he had done to her? *It was unthinkable that he possessed the nerve*, she thought to herself, as they made their way home.

Any feelings she may have had for Mr Keeling were soon supplanted by one she did not dare express. If he was in London, was she in danger of seeing him again?

Chapter 16

The Sutherlands' ball was one of the highlights of the season, according to Mrs Talridge who was anxiously coaching Lavinia and Charlotte about their hosts. They were an older couple who, according to Mrs Talridge, occupied a prominent place in London society. She also assured her granddaughter and Charlotte that their hosts were considered by many to be amongst the most well-known and sought after of the old London families. The Sutherlands were not country-born gentry, nor were they titled, but they were well known, and their wealth was rumoured to date back to the Tudor period. Lavinia suspected that this rumour was the result of a carefully constructed image her hosts had created, as they did not live in fashionable Hyde Park or Kensington. The Sutherlands chose to remain in permanent residence in an enormous brick and stone mansion situated along the river, a relic of the economically optimistic and expansive age.

Although Mr Sutherland and his wife were not of the peerage, it was rumoured that noble blood ran through the Sutherland lineage. Mrs Talridge favoured her young companions with a tale of a rakish young Henry the Eighth and a certain lady-in-waiting having produced the very first of the Sutherland line. As shocking as such a tale was, it was generally considered to be part of the mystique of the Sutherlands, as was their enormous largesse and holdings.

They were said to own entire neighbourhoods in London and as many enormous shares in merchant shipping as to make them the object of envy of many a count or duke.

Mrs Talridge explained that, for this reason, invitations to their stately home were considered prized possessions, even amongst the noteworthy members of the Ton.

As the carriage slowed to a stop in front of the great house, Mrs Talridge warned that all manner and class of society would be in attendance as the Sutherlands were known to consort with merchants and nobility alike. There may even be politicians, Mrs Talridge said, as a footman in Tudor livery opened the door of the carriage.

Within minutes, Mrs Talridge had led her granddaughter and her companion into the enormous great hall of the residence, a house, Lavinia observed, that resembled a fortress. As she passed footmen and servants dressed in old fashioned livery, she tried not to giggle. From the banners displayed on the walls and the impressive array of suits of armour, there could be no doubt that the Sutherlands wished to display their lengthy heritage in a not so subtle manner.

Charlotte leaned in close to Lavinia and whispered, "This house is medieval! I expect a knight in his armour to come riding through the hall at any moment!"

Lavinia laughed, as they joined her grandmother in the reception line. Upon her introduction to the Sutherlands, she was struck by the appearance of the couple. Mr Sutherland was dressed as a Tudor gentleman, complete with hose and a feathered cap. His wife, while not wearing a ruffed collar or a farthingale, was dressed in a contemporary fashion while still harkening back to the historical era. She was adorned in rows of pearls over a wide lace collar, which complimented the tailoring of her dress that comprised a long-waisted bodice and split skirt. Lavinia quickly glanced at the other guests, wondering if the ball was meant to be a costumed affair. She was relieved to discover that the costuming, like the footmen in their old style of livery, were merely eccentricities of the Sutherlands.

The Sutherlands were joined by their older children – a daughter dressed in crimson and gold, and a son who was wearing regimental red. Lavinia barely recalled either of them as her grandmother ushered them through the line in a rapid fashion. Once out of the Sutherlands' presence Mrs Talridge explained, "Did you see how Mrs Sutherland had her daughter dressed? I have never understood their obsession with the past... You would think we were attending court with Queen Elizabeth, to look at them."

"I can only presume that the rumour regarding the origin of the Sutherlands is true?" asked Lavinia.

Mrs Talridge made a clucking sound as she said silently, "You would think so. The staff and the hall have but one purpose and that is to remind all of the London that the Sutherlands have no need for the approval of modern society."

"Then why are so many of society here?"

"Lavinia, the Sutherlands are eccentric. They like to present themselves as near-royalty, but they are wealthy, no matter how strange they may be."

Lavinia did not mean to sound impertinent, but she was overwhelmed by the enormous crowd that swarmed all around her. "Is that why we are here tonight, because of their wealth?"

"We are here, because their son is unmarried. A family with their pedigree and their wide assortment of social connections may not object to any questionable details regarding a perspective match," Mrs Talridge explained.

"Is the son, Mr Sutherland, is he a captain?" Charlotte asked as she glanced towards the receiving line.

"He is a captain and a well-regarded young man. Do not allow his parents' preference for outlandish costumes to mar any judgement you may have. The son is amiable, educated, and a capable officer. It is because of his presence that I insisted we come to this ball."

"A captain... how splendid for you," Charlotte said to Lavinia.

"There are so many women here... it seems like every eligible young woman in all of London must be here tonight... how will he notice me?" Lavinia asked, as she strained to get a better look at the younger Mr Sutherland.

"He will notice you — of that you have my assurance. I have it on very good authority that he shall ask you to dance, before the evening is over," Mrs Talridge whispered with a knowing smile.

"You do not mean that you have been meddling about and playing the role of match-maker for me, do you?" Lavinia said to her grandmother.

"My dear child, that is my sole reason for coming to London. I have vowed that you will be settled — and settled you shall be. Smile, and look like you are perfectly content, for the reception line is at an end...

here he comes now... you have been properly introduced, so there is no impediment to your accepting his offer to dance," Mrs Talridge said to Lavinia as all three women greeted the young captain.

It did not escape Lavinia's notice that Captain Sutherland gazed upon the features of Charlotte for longer than was strictly necessary. Without any hint of embarrassment that his attentions had been firmly placed on the lovely Charlotte, he turned to Lavinia.

"Miss Talridge, it would be my greatest honour if you were to dance with me," he said firmly.

"Captain Sutherland, I would be delighted," Lavinia answered (although she wondered if she should be delighted to be dancing with a man who preferred the countenance of her companion).

"Shall we? The musicians are just beginning a Scottish reel." Captain Sutherland led Lavinia through the crowd towards the ballroom.

The room was glowing with candlelight. Enormous chandeliers hung from the ceiling, illuminating the dancers assembled beneath. On a dais at the end of the room, a group of musicians, dressed in Elizabethan costume, were striking the first notes as the dancers formed their lines. Lavinia studied the captain as they waited for the dance to begin. In his regimentals, he was a dashing figure even if he was not a handsome man. His hair was brown, in a nondescript shade that was of a medium hue, his eyes were small and close together, and his features were ill-defined with a propensity towards corpulence. She wondered how he would appear in an afternoon jacket and breeches. Would he appear plain and unamusing, despite the cost of his attire? As Lavinia danced with the captain, she privately chided herself for her criticism of his appearance. If she had worn any other dress than the rose ball gown, that evening, would she not be less pleasing in her appearance? It was terrible to judge the captain by his appearance alone, especially when he had proven himself to be nothing less than a gentleman in their brief acquaintance.

"Miss Talridge, is it the custom in Yorkshire to not converse during a reel?" he asked as they moved in time to the music.

"My apologies, Captain Sutherland."

"There is no need to apologise, I do hope you are enjoying the evening."

"I am overwhelmed, as I have never been to a ball here, at your home. It is an occasion, and I do enjoy it greatly."

"My father would be pleased that you think so. I find the whole affair to be tedious, similarly dinners and balls. I prefer less formal pursuits."

"Do you enjoy hunting? Or perhaps the theatre?" Lavinia asked in a perfunctory manner. Captain Sutherland was attempting to make conversation and the least she could do was to make a similar effort.

"Neither. I enjoy drills and life at camp... That may strike you as peculiar, but I am an officer through and through. If I had my way, I would remain in the army until I made the rank of colonel."

"That is a noble ambition, sir. What will you do now that the war is at an end?"

"I shall resign my commission, I suppose. My father is eager that I join him in business, but I have no wish to bore you with such details. I must remember that ladies are not accustomed to discussing matters pertaining to finances and money at a ball. What shall we discuss instead? How do you find London?"

"I find it to be entertaining," Lavinia replied as she chided herself for lying, wishing to say that she found it to be noisy, overcrowded, and filled with poor people who desperately needed assistance.

"Entertaining? I suppose it would be for a woman from Yorkshire. I am told that you have not been long amongst London society. Is this your first season?"

"How curious that you know so much about me."

"It is not curious, not when you consider that my mother and your grandmother are well-acquainted," he explained.

"As I presume they wish us to be," Lavinia said under her breath.

"Did you say something?"

"No, not at all," Lavinia replied as the music came to an end.

"Shall we have a glass of punch?" Captain Sutherland asked as he held out his arm to Lavinia.

"Yes, I would like that, thank you," she answered as he placed her hand on the crimson material of his sleeve.

The captain was attentive, he smiled as she spoke, and he asked her questions in a polite manner. She was not sure what his opinion of her might be but being in his company was like being with a companion who did not disagree, nor passionately agree, with any opinion, Lavinia thought, as they sat together in the ballroom sipping punch from glasses.

"Would you be willing to dance with me again, this evening? It would be an honour to escort you in a cotillion or a reel, Miss Talridge," Captain Sutherland said as he placed the empty glass on the tray of nearby footman.

Lavinia was surprised that she did not find his offer objectionable. "Yes, Captain Sutherland, a second dance with you would be delightful."

Finishing her punch, her empty glass soon joined his on the tray, and he led her back to the floor. She could feel the scrutiny of some of the older ladies in the ballroom, especially the same ladies her grandmother consorted with amongst the Ton – ladies such as Lady Cavendish and Lady Whitfield whose stares Lavinia tried to ignore.

"You notice them too?" Captain Sutherland asked smilingly as he bent towards her.

"You mean–?"

"Yes, the older women. They are the old guard... the guardians of society here in London. They and their young cohorts call themselves the Ton. If you ask me, they make much of themselves... I prefer to take people as I meet them... Have I shocked you?"

Lavinia laughed, a genuine laugh that was not disingenuous in any way. "You have not shocked me, Captain Sutherland. I have opinions of my own that are just as shocking, and perhaps one day I will share them with you."

"I look forward to that day," he answered.

Lavinia was more and more pleasantly surprised by this young man, who was now leading her to the next dance. He was not much older than she was – perhaps he was twenty-five years of age, but she found his personality charming. He was wealthy, but he spoke in a good-natured manner that one might find amongst tradesmen and merchants, and to her astonishment, she found that she was rather enjoying his company. As she was reflecting on his attributes, which surpassed any shortcomings in his appearance, she was confronted by a sight that caused her suddenly to wish that she was somewhere else entirely.

Walking across the ballroom, with a young woman at his side, was none other than Mr Keeling.

Lavinia realised with a startle that Captain Sutherland was lining up to dance. She stopped in her tracks and thought about offering the gentleman an excuse not to dance this time, but she could not arrive at a suitable reason. If she claimed to be taken ill, a doctor may be summoned. If she rushed away without saying a word, Captain Sutherland may be led to think that she found his company objectionable. On the other hand, if she stayed and danced, perhaps she could avoid all contact with Mr Keeling, and then make her escape when the music was at an end?

Settling on that course of action, she joined Captain Sutherland, thankful that Mr Keeling was positioned further down the line of couples, which meant that she would see him in passing, but not be required to acknowledge him. Smiling and staring at her companion, she refused to look in the direction of Mr Keeling. She prayed that he had not seen her – a prayer that she knew was selfish, but necessary.

The musicians played a lively reel, and Lavinia tried to concentrate on Captain Sutherland as she laughed at anything humorous (or not as humorous) he said and tried to conceal her discomfort at the nearness of Mr Keeling. She was also busy trying to think of a perfectly acceptable reason to make a hasty exit from the ballroom. Perhaps, she could seek out Charlotte? Or join her grandmother? Or–?

She was so entirely consumed by her plans for a departure from the festivities of dancing, that she was caught completely by surprise, and she glanced towards Mr Keeling. He was glancing at her, his green eyes gazing in her direction in a bold and unapologetic fashion. He did not bother to look away – but Lavinia did, as her cheeks burned crimson with embarrassment. How *audacious* he was to stare at her so, after the indignity she had suffered at his hands! She was so preoccupied, that when the dance came to an end, she was unprepared to carry out her plan. She stood in the company of Captain Sutherland, breathless from the exertion of dancing a lively reel, and trying to recall exactly how she had planned to make her egress. She realised, all too late, that her inaction was a costly error.

"Have you been introduced to my fellow officer, Major George Keeling? He fought with me under Wellington," Captain Sutherland said as he nodded to Mr Keeling.

Lavinia did not quite know what to say. She felt the overwhelming urge to run away, but she was unable to behave any differently in her present situation, which kept her at Captain Sutherland's side, as he led her towards Mr Keeling and his companion.

"I... do not know," Lavinia said in a tone she was certain that Captain Sutherland did not hear over the din of voices.

"If you haven't met him, you should do so at once! He is to be commended as he has been decorated for his valour... He won't tell you about it, but my father considers him to be amongst his guests of honour this evening... Here we are, Major Keeling at last," Captain Sutherland said as he nodded to the man.

The young lady at Mr Keeling's side greeted Captain Sutherland and Lavinia with a wary smile, as Captain Sutherland went about the duty of a host, making the proper introductions. Lavinia wanted to speak up and to tell him that she was well-acquainted with

Mr Keeling, although she was unaware that he had become a major. Despite the presence of the young woman, whom Lavinia discovered to be a real lady (the daughter of the earl of Montrose), Lavinia felt the gaze of Mr, now Major, Keeling upon her.

She did not speak to him, other than what was necessary, and he did not say anything else to her. When Lavinia could not bear to be in his presence a moment longer, she mumbled an excuse and quickly curtseyed, leaving her host and his company behind.

She did not look back and wished she could be as far away from Major Keeling as she could manage. Her anger rose as she considered his audacity. How dare he look at her as he once had! She was no longer that little insecure girl she had once been, she said to herself, as she raced (rather insecurely) through the hall. Lavinia stopped when she found herself by the fireside, standing beside a coat of armour under the stairs.

Desperate for a private, quiet corner in which to collect her thoughts, Lavinia searched for a hiding place and hoped she had found one here. She could not face him again, not ever. How was she to control her temper and to say what she truly felt to him? She was frustrated that he should arrive at the ball and ruin it for her, especially since she was having a perfectly splendid time in the presence of Captain Sutherland? Why did he always have to wreck everything? She was pondering that very question when she saw *him*. He was striding through the hall alone, his female companion nowhere to be seen. Lavinia closed her eyes and hoped that he would not see her, however, upon opening her eyes, she realised that it was too late.

He was walking towards her.

"Miss Talridge," he bowed as he said her name.

"Major Keeling," she replied without a trace of warmth.

"I have caused you distress... I apologise."

Lavinia was not sure to what he was referring – the ball or the wedding, so she stared at him, unsure how to respond to the man she loathed.

"Lavinia!" Mrs Talridge spoke her name sharply as Lavinia and Major Keeling turned to face the woman.

Mrs Talridge was unapologetic about her sudden intrusion. With only a cursory greeting to Major Keeling, she rescued Lavinia from his presence, whisking her away before he had much to say about it. Lavinia was appreciative of her grandmother's interruption, even if it meant being introduced to another young gentleman in the ballroom. This man, Lord Burwickshire, was short, his face was round, and he smiled a bit too easily as he discussed the merits of hunting in Derbyshire – but none of that really seemed to matter to Lavinia as her mind remained deeply distraught by what had happened.

By the end of the evening, and after two more introductions to gentlemen who had been selected by Mrs Talridge, Lavinia was quite fatigued. With so many promising gentlemen asking to pay social calls at their earliest convenience, she was disturbed that she could not think of any man other than Major Keeling. She had not seen him after the incident under the stairs, but she had the distinct feeling that he was never far away.

Lavinia could not help it, and even though her own curiosity in this regard bothered her, she was curious about what he might have said, had he not been interrupted.

Chapter 17

"I will not permit Mr Keeling in my house," Mrs Talridge exclaimed as she fanned herself furiously by the fireside. "Nor will I receive him in any manner!"

The fire was blazing in the drawing room in the chill of the morning following the Sutherlands' ball. The room was slightly cold and the fire roaring in the fireplace was not needed to warrant Mrs Talridge's furious fanning. Lavinia suspected that the fanning was an extension of Mrs Talridge's disgusted expression, a display of her distaste for Major Keeling and his unexpected presence in London.

"I do not think that you should be concerned about receiving him, since I have no doubt that seeing him at the ball was a mere coincidence," Lavinia replied.

Charlotte glanced at Lavinia in a way that signalled an unspoken comment (she suspected that Charlotte was silently hinting at the brief interlude in the park). How thankful Lavinia was at that moment that Charlotte was a loyal friend and companion, as neither of them brought up that incident.

"I have no interest in receiving him, but I may have no choice. He is a war hero! He was decorated for bravery! I cannot account for his bravery, but I have it on very good authority that Wellington himself is said to be pressing Major Keeling to remain in his service. It is unthinkable that he should be the same man... the very same man who humiliated this family," Mrs Talridge continued as she dropped her fan in her lap.

"Might we return to Yorkshire?" offered Lavinia, hopeful that her grandmother would agree. "He was not spoken of in any of the circles there, and I doubt he is received by his family or we would have heard that he had returned to his home."

"How can we return to Claxton Hall? Not now, when your prospects are brightening. I am impressed that the ball went as I planned, even if he was there to dampen our spirits," her grandmother replied.

"Mrs Talridge, if I may make a suggestion," said Charlotte. "Is it not impossible to believe that he may not attempt any contact after last night's rejection of his apology?"

"If he had any decency and respect for me, and for my dear Lavinia, he would remain far away. I do not think he will venture to be so forward as to take advantage of our previous acquaintance, but I do wish he had stayed gone and forgotten. What are we to do? What if he does presume upon the introduction made by Captain Sutherland? I am caught in a terrible position as I have no wish to speak to him, but he is accepted by the Sutherlands. Lady Cavendish was saying last night that he was accepted at her home and also that of Lady Whitfield. It *is* intolerable, I tell you, the idea that I should have to speak to him politely, when I have no wish to speak to him at all."

Mrs Talridge was in a perfect state of vexation. Charlotte did as she was often called upon to do, and that was to soothe her employer's nerves as Lavinia listened to the patter of rain against the panes of glass in the windows. With the damp weather set in for the day, there would be no promenade that day along the walking paths in Hyde

Park, if the paths were muddy. Sighing, as she stared out the window, she watched a messenger arrive at the curb. He rushed through the rain and up the stairs as she wondered who could be sending a messenger at this early hour. The ball was over but a few hours ago, and most of London society would be sleeping. She was awake, true, and so were her grandmother and Charlotte, but that was because of the shock that seeing Major Keeling had caused.

The footman knocked at the door of the drawing room to bring the newly arrived message.

Mrs Talridge frowned as she read the contents, her brow furrowing into lines and deep wrinkles that signalled her unhappiness. She clenched her jaw and then exhaled sharply as she replied, "Tell the messenger that, yes, we shall attend tea this afternoon."

"Mrs Talridge?" Charlotte asked as the footman left the room, softly closing the door.

"How audacious! Never have I experienced such an unchecked display of effrontery... I am appalled that he would think that he could address either of us in public or, I fear, make an attempt to come into my home after what he did to Lavinia."

"Grandmother, please tell me that message was not from Major Keeling," Lavinia whispered.

"How am I to lie to you? It was concerning none other than the man himself. We will be forced to see him this very day, in the afternoon... but have no worries, my dear Lavinia, I intend to ensure that our visit will not be a long one. We may be forced to speak to a hero of the war, but we do not have to make him feel we have forgiven him!"

"He's coming here?" Lavinia exclaimed.

"Not yet, but I fear he may take our cooperation in the matter as a sign that he *is* welcome. We have been invited to tea at Lady Whitfield's this afternoon and in the message, she has informed me that he is to be counted amongst the guests... How infuriating... how can she feign ignorance that this was the same person who dealt so terribly with us? I would refuse the invitation, but I cannot."

"Has the messenger gone? May I send word that I am too ill to attend?" Lavinia asked as she rushed to the door.

"No, my dear, if you send word that you are ill, you shall have to spend the remainder of the season doing just that. If he is received by Lady Whitfield, as he was received by the Sutherlands, then there can be no doubt that he shall be present at every ball for the rest of the season. We shall go to tea, but we shall not be polite to a scoundrel. Never that. I am certain we can say as little to him as if he were a person of no consequence... We shall endure this humiliation as best we can."

Lavinia did not wish to endure any more embarrassment at the hands of Major Keeling. She could see the determined look on her grandmother's face and Charlotte appeared to be concerned in her own way, showing a frown on her beautiful features. If Lavinia had these two women at her side, perhaps she could face him and be done with the matter?

After the morning's excitement, Lavinia willingly shuttered herself away in the music room, while her grandmother received cards and visitors. She did not have the slightest interest in her music, but she did want time alone to think. How was she to face him again? Neglecting her music, she sat at the piano. Her eyes were fixed on the pages in front of her, but her mind drifted away to the parade of eligible gentlemen that she had met at the ball. She would prefer to see any of them at tea rather than to sit prim and proper, as a group of fashionable ladies fawned over Major Keeling, the decorated war hero. She wondered if they would be doing quite as much fawning if it were their daughters who had suffered embarrassment on their wedding day.

The rain continued to fall as she left the piano, to seek out a place by the window where she could watch the drops splattering against the glass. She was relieved that she did not have to become his wife, so why was she still angered after all this time? Was it the embarrassment? Was it his dismissal of her, that she was not worth as much as a note explaining the reason why he had left her?

She thought of taking to her bed, and of convincing her grandmother that she was far too ill to attend tea at Lady Whitfield's, but she would not be a coward. She had shown herself to be cowardly at the ball, and she would *not* run away again. *Let him be the one who feels embarrassed, let him be the one who is forced to leave her company,* she thought. That would be the only way she could conquer him once and for all.

With that resolved, she sat down at her piano again, practicing the music until she felt satisfied with her efforts. How quickly the time passed that day, until she was dressed in her finest afternoon dress, a confection of blue and lilac with a matching pelisse and bonnet. She was ready to face Major Keeling and a room full of women who were all members of the Ton. Charlotte was trembling, but Lavinia suspected it was because of her concern for how Mrs Talridge would react to seeing the scoundrel amongst her own set of acquaintances.

As they arrived at the stately town house of Lady Whitfield, Charlotte confessed that she would not be surprised if Mrs Talridge threw her tea in the major's face. Lavinia could not disagree – she too wondered how her grandmother would accept the man who had insulted her.

It promised to be quite an afternoon.

"Mrs Talridge, Miss Talridge, Miss Fenwick, how good of you to have come to tea... I do hope you won't mind that I have invited a limited number of guests this afternoon," Lady Whitfield greeted them in the drawing room.

Lavinia was immediately struck by the quiet in the room and wondered if they were early for tea, or if Lady Whitfield was correct that she was not hosting a large affair? Charlotte remained at Lavinia's side as they were ushered to their seats, and her grandmother took a place near the fireside.

"I find a small guest list makes the conversation far more stimulating," Mrs Talridge replied.

Tea was prepared – a full service, with all the trimmings of cakes and sandwiches, was laid out, but there were no other guests present, except for them and Lady Whitfield.

"My daughter will be joining us and Captain Sutherland, and Major Keeling will be here at any moment. I am certain that you have arrived at the reason for my invitation?" Lady Whitfield said as she glanced towards Lavinia.

"Lady Whitfield, shall we speak plainly, since we are not in the company of other guests?" Mrs Talridge said. "I do not wish to spoil your tea, but this is a pressing matter."

"That is precisely the reason I have asked my other guests to arrive a quarter of an hour after you. I know it seems terribly inconvenient to them, but I have a matter of urgency to discuss and I did not wish to make it a public one," Lady Whitfield remarked.

For a brief moment, Lavinia wondered if Major Keeling had told Lady Whitfield about her past. Would she be told that the daughter of a seamstress had no place in polite society? Would she be asked to leave this house after suffering from the embarrassment of having the unfortunate details of her birth made public?

"The matter, if I may speak indelicately, concerns Major Keeling. He has told me something that I find startling. In fact, I was astonished that he would tell me of it, and even more astonished that he sought to enlist my aid," Lady Whitfield began as she leaned in close to Mrs Talridge.

"If this concerns my granddaughter, there is nothing to say except that your guest left *her* on their wedding day," Mrs Talridge blurted out. "He showed her not the slightest respect, when she had done nothing to deserve the indignity. He did not care to explain himself or to make his excuses, as a gentleman might, and behaved in an alarming manner – one that has been addressed by my solicitor. His father does not receive him and neither does anyone in Yorkshire."

"I know perfectly well what he did," Lady Whitfield huffed, "He confessed to me what you have recounted... As you have spoken of him in the past also, I am well acquainted with his failure to act in a proper fashion towards Miss Talridge, but there is much to be considered in the present that may change your opinion."

"If I may... I know it is not my place to question you, but may I ask how you can champion such a man?" Mrs Talridge asked, her stare becoming rather narrow as she peered at their hostess.

Lady Whitfield was undeterred, "No, my dear Mrs Talridge, it is well within your rights to question my reception of him. It may seem monstrous that I have done so, and I must admit that I was unwilling to speak to Major Keeling since he is the second son of Viscount of Wharton and hardly a gentleman of worth, except for his connection to his father. However, I was acquainted with his family and his mother many years ago. I was reintroduced to the gentleman at the home of the Duke of Rathington, a general who served in the last campaign of the war, and I was surprised to find that Major Keeling was honourable, having served with distinction under none other than General Wellington. His leadership was credited with saving the lives of countless men... If it were not for his powerful allies and his meritorious service, I would not be sitting here having this conversation with you. I do hope you can understand why I have chosen to receive him."

Lavinia listened in horror and fascination. It was too much to consider, and she felt suddenly light-headed. As the two older women exchanged varying opinions, she was unprepared for the next striking statement from Lady Whitfield.

"I was not prepared when he came to me... he enlisted my aid when he discovered that we were acquainted, Mrs Talridge. How could I say no to the request of a man who may have helped us win the war? How, I ask you, could I deny his request in good conscience?" Lady Whitfield explained.

Mrs Talridge frowned, but she appeared to be softening under the pressure that was being exerted by Lady Whitfield. Lavinia was pleased that her grandmother had held her own for as long as she dared. It was unusual to question the actions of a lady of rank and title, and Lavinia knew all too well that Mrs Talridge had done so at her peril. Resisting the urge to shower her grandmother with grateful affection, she listened as Mrs Talridge reluctantly agreed to allow Major Keeling to speak to Lavinia during the tea.

"He wants to make amends. He has explained his actions to me, and although I am not in agreement with his handling of the situation, I cannot fault his sincerity. He behaved reprehensibly, but he has expressed his deepest regret to me, and he shall do the same, I am certain, to you and your granddaughter. Are we to hold him, a hero of the war, accountable for the mistakes of his youth?" Lady Whitfield ended her speech as the footman announced the arrival of the other guests.

Lavinia wanted to reach out for Charlotte's hand, but chose instead to remain as she was, rigid in her posture, as one who was bravely facing a challenge.

Captain Sutherland greeted her with cheer, and Lady Whitfield's daughter was quiet and amiable. Major Keeling bowed humbly in her presence and did not flinch as she expected he might. Instead, he looked at her in the same intense way that he had done before their ill-fated engagement.

"Miss Talridge, it is a privilege and an honour to be speaking with you again," he said to Lavinia.

Lavinia swallowed, as she dared not look at him for too long. A flood of emotions washed over her. She wanted to scream at him, and to yell, but that was not acceptable in polite society. She did not know what to say, but she could not allow herself to embarrass her grandmother, at least not in front of Lady Whitfield or the charming Captain Sutherland. When she looked at the young captain, she was struck with an overwhelming sense of mortification. How much did *he* know of her past? Did *he* know how poorly she was treated by Major Keeling?

"I understand that you may not want to speak with me," the major replied.

Lavinia knew that she was being observed, "We may speak, Major Keeling... if you insist."

"I do not deserve an audience with you, but I seek one. Shall I be allowed a few minutes to tell you how humbly I wish to apologise?" he asked in a calm and sincere way.

Lavinia did not know how she should reply, but she knew that Lady Whitfield was championing Major Keeling and that her grandmother didn't seem to offer any objection. Nodding her head, he asked if she would join him on the other side of the drawing room, where they might speak in private, but under the watchful eye of her grandmother. The request, just like the invitation to tea, was highly unusual, and Lavinia could offer no objection, publicly. Privately she was filled with reasons not to speak to him or listen to anything he had to say.

Across the drawing room, and beside a bay window overlooking a tranquil scene of an orderly London street, Lavinia and Major Keeling sat down together. She was nervous in his presence, and anxious that she would bolt from him at the slightest provocation.

He sat across from her, and his eyes searched her face steadily, as he spoke.

"Miss Talridge... I would call you Lavinia as we were once better acquainted, but I know that time has passed... I want to thank you for allowing me to speak, as candidly as I must, to you."

"Major Keeling, since there is no danger of our being overheard, I should warn you that I am listening to you out of a sense of duty to my grandmother," Lavinia's voice was cold. "You may be an officer and a hero, but I know you for who you are. I have not forgotten your ill treatment of me."

"How I have wanted to make amends, but I was on the continent. I do not offer excuses... I could have sent a letter to you at any time, but I did not think you would read it."

"You could have sent me a letter on the day of the wedding!" Lavinia's voice broke, but she regained her composure quickly, "You could have spared me the disgrace and not agreed to marry me at all."

"I tried to do that, but my father has a will that is like iron... He would not listen to me or anyone else... I was a fool to agree to his terms – that I should marry you when I knew I would make you miserable and drive myself to madness."

"I would drive you to madness, is that what you are suggesting? How cruel you are. I wonder if Lady Whitfield knows you as well as she thinks she does."

"*You* would not drive me to madness, it would be my *own* will... my *own* need to do something with my life other than to marry a woman chosen by my father. I wanted to serve in the army. I have felt the call to the military life ever since I was a boy, wanting to follow the example of my uncle who was a colonel in the army."

Lavinia was silent for a few moments.

"I wonder, Major Keeling, if you would have felt the same way if I were an heiress, when you abandoned me? How terribly you treated me back then, when it seemed that you thought I was beneath you.

You behaved in my presence as though I was far below your respect."

"It pains me to recall my treatment of you. I was playing the role of the dutiful son and no more. I was foolish in my cowardice. If I had taken a stand against my father's plans for me, then you would have been spared the humiliation I brought upon you."

Lavinia glared at him, "I cannot trust a word you have to say to me. How am I to know that this sudden show of repentance is not brought on by my change of fortune? I was the lowly daughter of a seamstress when I met you, and you made no attempt to conceal your disapproval with the arrangement of our marriage."

"You are within your rights to criticise me and to scold me for the injustice I brought down upon you. If I were suddenly to inherit great wealth, I too would be hasty to assume that any alteration in the behaviour of past acquaintances was inspired by greed and avarice. Allow me to assure you, Miss Talridge, that I do not seek your wealth *nor* your hand in marriage."

Lavinia fell silent again.

"Then what do you want, Major Keeling?"

"I seek your forgiveness. I cannot express my deepest regret, in words, that I behaved as I did to you. You were young, and you were honest and trusting and I betrayed that trust. Furthermore, I treated you as though you did not deserve my name or to become my wife. I ask that you understand the reason I behaved as I did. It was my father I wished to strike against – not you. How could I marry you, when I had different aspirations, and wanted my life and my death to have meaning? I wanted to wear the regimentals and to do my duty to my country, as my uncle had years before. If I had been trapped under the weight of an arranged marriage to the granddaughter of a local gentlewoman, I would have felt my life was entirely useless, and that I had failed my king and country."

"Why did you not say that to me? You had countless opportunities to appear to me in person or to send a note, but instead, you left me to face all of Yorkshire society as a woman who was not worthy of marriage to you." Lavinia struggled to suppress her rising indignation.

Major Keeling nodded. "There can be no doubt that I handled the situation poorly, and it pains me to think of my actions. I will unburden myself to you, and tell you the truth of what happened, as it may help you to understand that it was not your fault, nor was the slight meant against you. The night before the wedding, I could no longer contain my frustration. I went to my father, and we argued. He threatened to cast me off, and to disown me if I did not marry you. Being proud and arrogant, I left that night – penniless, alone, and without enough money to secure a commission. My brother lent me the sum I needed to become an officer, and with his help, and the connections afforded to me because of my family name, I was accepted as an officer."

"You could have sent word to me that you had left me on our wedding, to join the army. Why did you not tell me that, or make it known in Yorkshire that you chose to become an officer? Did you care so little for me or my good name?"

"Forgive me... I did not know how to write to you the painful truth that my ambition and my desire to prove myself on the battlefield meant more to me than you or your happiness." He looked into Lavinia's eyes, "I was selfish, I know that now. I thought only of myself and my mission to serve as an officer, and I presumed, after our meeting in the chapel, that you would be relieved that I had not followed through with our wedding. I told myself that you felt as I did, and that you were marrying me because of a sense of duty and nothing more."

Lavinia felt a twinge of understanding. The chapel. She *was* relieved that she had not had to marry him. He had understood her position as well as his own, with a clarity that left her temporarily speechless, until she recalled how he had spoken to her and how he had treated her.

"I can forgive you for your sudden departure, but what of your ill treatment of me? You never behaved as if I was deserving of your attention, but rather treated me as a person who belonged in your scullery, not in your drawing room."

Major Keeling did not disagree, "I am that person I was no longer. The war and my time amongst London society has taught me my place in this world. I am a second son. I stand to inherit not a piece of property nor a grand estate. Since I returned to London, I have existed on my officer's salary and the kindness of my wealthy friends."

"Why are you telling me this? You have no reason to confide in me."

"I wish to confide in you, because I have the feeling that you may be the only person with whom I may be entirely myself. You knew me at my worst and yet here you are granting me an opening to make amends."

"I have not granted you that opportunity... my grandmother has obliged me to do so," Lavinia said softly.

"I am grateful for her generosity, and perhaps I may benefit from yours in the future?"

"In what manner?"

"I ask that you allow me the chance to earn your respect – nothing more. I am not ashamed that I went to war, and that I chose to become an officer, rather than remain in Yorkshire to fulfil my father's demands. What brings shame to me is the reckless manner with which I chose to pursue the officer's uniform. I will not plead, for I am a proud man, but I ask that you consider accepting my regret that, in the pursuit of honour on the continent, I behaved dishonourably towards you."

Lavinia was unsure of what to say to him, or how to answer his request. When they were engaged to be wed, he had barely spoken to her – he was never amiable to her, nor did he behave in any way other than to assert his position, which was far above her own. Glancing at the small group assembled by the fireside, she looked closely at him, and studied him in earnest, before she spoke, "I see that I am left with little choice in the matter. You have enlisted the assistance of none other than Lady Whitfield. Who am I to go against her championing of you? For my grandmother's sake, I am left with no other recourse than to deal fairly and amicably with you.... If you seek politeness, then I can agree to that, but I assure you that it is not what I would wish. If you desire friendship and amity, then that will not be gained easily."

"Politeness that is forced by my connections, may be all I will be granted, but I will not rest until I have righted the indignity I inflicted upon you." His voice was calm and straightforward.

"You may earn my respect for your heroics in battle, but you shall never earn my trust of you or your motives. My dowry and estate are not as meagre as they once were, and you shall never convince me that you seek my esteem for any cause other than greed," Lavinia added.

"You are right to distrust me, for I have not earned the right to be trusted. Your fortunes have changed your position in the world, and it is for that reason that I declare that I possess no designs upon them. I know that I have no reason to hope that you will believe that I hold your interest as far surpassing my own, but I wish to offer you a gift."

Indignantly, Lavinia huffed as she replied, "A gift? We are not well enough acquainted, nor are we amiable. It is improper that you should offer me a gift which would indebt me to you."

"No, not that kind of gift – not a gift that you can hold in your hands, but one that is, hopefully, far more useful. As I failed to protect you from ridicule in Yorkshire, by my actions, I would like to offer you my unconditional friendship, my advocacy, my connections, and my protection amongst society."

Lavinia was quick to reply, "Protection? You mean I am in need of protection?" Despite her question, Lavinia sensed what the major was referring to. She knew what was rumored on the streets. She was what many liked to call a 'prize to be sought'. A woman sought by gentlemen who had no other means of making their fortunes. "You mean by gentlemen much like yourself?" she added.

"I will not conceal that my fortunes in the world are much reduced, while yours have risen considerably, but as I mentioned earlier, rest assured – your wealth is of no interest to me, nor do I offer marriage to you. Be careful to trust a title, or an elevated connection amongst the fashionable people here in town," Major Keeling said in a low voice as he glanced at the hostess of the tea. "I have seen the habits of many a young man who appears to be steadfast and earnest, but who in fact gambles or associates with those of low reputation. I have been amongst those gentlemen who would value you for your estate and squander your money on their dissipated and dissolute lives while you are left in misery."

"I am aware that society is infected with these men of poor moral character. However, I am confident that my grandmother would never allow me to make a mistake that might cost me so dearly," Lavinia replied, as she lifted her chin in a haughty manner.

"Mrs Talridge is a formidable woman, and both her wisdom and her tenacity do her credit, but I do not think her agents would easily be welcomed amongst the circles that I have fallen among, unfortunately. I am seen as an opportunist by some, much to my despair. As the second son of a viscount, with only my army pension to sustain me, I have considered what course of action awaits me. I must marry my fortune or resign myself to a life of modest expense."

Lavinia was surprised by his honest words, "But you are not an opportunist and are not amongst those men I should be careful of?"

"No, I am not, nor will I ever be, but I have often been considered to be amongst the ranks of these men, and I am by necessity. It is impossible to ignore these scoundrels at the tables of the clubs I frequent, or to avoid them as they make their wagers. I have been pursued by spinsters and old women alike, because they see me as a man in need of a bride, in my present circumstances, and it gives me no pleasure. I shall remain in London for a fortnight, but then I am bound for Yorkshire."

"You are going home, then? Before the season is at an end?"

"I am going home. My father may not receive me, but I expect a welcome from my brother. You are not the only wrong I intend to right, thus I'm going to return to Yorkshire and to Cotes Cross to make amends."

Lavinia was no longer as angry as she had been at the beginning of the discussion. Instead, she felt curious about this man who sat across from her. He was not as humble as he might have been, and his shoulders were not slumped in supplication. He appeared as he always had, proud and confident, but there was something new in his manner, and he was aware that he had behaved abominably. She did not know if she could trust him, that would not be easily granted, and she searched her mind for reason to reject his words but could not find one.

"Major Keeling, if you have the opportunity to find out if a gentleman is moving in ... certain circles, what of you? How can I believe that you do not say such things to make yourself appear all the more favourable?"

"If I offer you my opinion, you may discount it. I hope you will understand that the news is honestly intended, in order to secure your happiness, and not my own."

"I do not know how to answer this request..."

"You should say no, you do not have to be amiable to me. One word of you is enough, and I will leave – I promise, you shall never see me again."

"Major Keeling, I am not su–"

"I did not cherish the chance I once had with you. In the war, I observed the equality of men fighting together on the field of battle. Officers such as myself may lead the men, but we all fight for the same cause, and for the same king. I have reason to see the world differently, and I no longer hold the same beliefs as I once did. Allow me to call on you, and you shall see a changed man before you."

Lavinia wanted to tell him no, and to reject his offer of friendship. She wanted to declare that she never wished to see him again, but that was her mind – a part of her was filled with an insatiable curiosity. How had this man transformed into the gentleman she saw in front of her? If he paid a call on her or walked at her side in Hyde Park, perhaps she might discern whether he was truthful, or if he was as villainous as she recalled.

"I had quite forgotten about a prior engagement," Mrs Talridge was making her excuses to Lady Whitfield.

Lavinia knew of no other engagements for the afternoon or evening, but she had felt the gaze of her grandmother's intense scrutiny during her time in Major Keeling's company. She was not surprised that her grandmother was as good as her word, and she was putting an end to Major Keeling's hopes for reconciliation.

As Lavinia said goodbye to Major Keeling and her hostess, as well as to the other small groups of guests, she glanced at Major Keeling, a question on her lips left unsaid.

Would he keep his word, she wondered, after he had broken it so disgracefully on their wedding day?

Chapter 18

Lavinia's first season in London was at an end, and she was not engaged. Her grandmother lamented this unhappy fact, but Lavinia did
not share her discontent. London society was not at all to Lavinia's
liking. Dancing at the balls was a joyful pastime, but the guests were
often crowded into rooms until conversation was nearly impossible.
The dinners were delicious, but the company was never certain, as
Lavinia was often seated with nearly perfect strangers. In the presence
of the Sutherlands and Lady Whitfield, Lavinia was never quite herself, and never able to speak her mind. During her weeks spent in London, she did meet many interesting men, but she learned from her
grandmother's research into their backgrounds that there were many
who were not suitable for matrimony.

Lavinia sat outside in the garden of Claxton Hall, enjoying the
warm breeze that was scented with jasmine and roses. The birds twit-
tered in the bushes along the hedgerow and in the boughs of the ancient oaks overhead, that shaded Lavinia and Charlotte. *How delightful it felt to be home again*, she thought, as she penned a letter to the
vicar. How delightful indeed, when she thought about seeing the
young vicar once again. He had promised to pay a visit in London, but
he never had, claiming a sickness had swept the village of Cotes Cross.
Not wanting to be overly eager, Lavinia had replied in her neat hand
that she was at home, once more, and would like to invite him to tea.
She wondered if it was slightly improper to invite a gentleman to tea,

but this was the vicar and he occupied a place in society not constricted by the usual dictates. As she worded the invitation, she wondered if she might also send a letter to Major Keeling.

How odd, Lavinia marvelled, that they were acquaintances, after all that had transpired between them. She thought of their last encounter in a drawing room in London where he was nearby, warning her of the lecherous intentions of an older married man. He had proven indispensable, and she was astonished to say that he had been as good as his word. She laughed when she thought of her grandmother's glares the time Major Keeling had warned Lavinia of the scoundrel's intention before her grandmother discovered the same news to be true. It seemed to Lavinia that, in the short time since Major Keeling had returned to their acquaintance, even her grandmother was beginning to scowl less in his presence – or did she imagine it?

When he had left London, Lavinia had missed his company, even if she did not wish to say it aloud.

"I wonder if we have received a letter or a message from Major Keeling? I have not written to him, but he surely must know we are home... I shall not forget to have a look through the mail."

Charlotte sighed heavily as she sat at the table opposite Lavinia. Lavinia finished the letter to the vicar and said, "Charlotte, you are not quite yourself, since we returned home. Was the journey too taxing for you?"

"No, it was not the journey. I do not mind riding in a carriage as well appointed as the one belonging to your grandmother."

"Then what has brought you to this state? Have you not missed the singing of our native birds, and the warmth of the sunshine on the hillsides?"

"I confess that Yorkshire is beautiful in summer, but I am not content, and I wish that it were otherwise."

"Is it London that you miss? The crowded streets, the drawing rooms filled with gossip and the men who mean to trap women such as me, with deviousness?"

Charlotte smiled, "I miss London, but not for the society."

Lavinia replied, "I dare say, you profess to not missing society, but there is the society of one gentleman whom you miss, is there not?"

Charlotte's rosy complexion turned a deeper shade of pink as she looked away, "I do not know whom you mean."

"Oh... let me take a guess... Could it be... a certain Captain Sutherland? I believe you captured his eye on his visits to our house."

"How shocking of you to imply that. He came to see you, and he may make a proposal by Christmas, if you are inclined to encourage him."

"He may make a proposal to me, but I fear he was enamoured by your beauty, my dear Charlotte! There is nothing shocking in that... the only thing that is shocking, is that I had no idea *you* held him in the same regard."

"My beauty is nothing to your estate," Charlotte answered.

"Perhaps we may do something about that arrangement? You have been a true and loyal friend for all these years. My grandmother would see nothing wrong with settling an amount for an annuity for your income."

"You are generous, but even an annuity would not settle a gentleman such as Captain Sutherland, and I am sure his family would never permit a marriage to a lady's companion such as myself, when he might have a woman of your fortune."

"But would *I* have him, knowing what you just told me?" Lavinia said as she watched an approaching footman walk along the garden path towards them.

"Ma'am, Mr Edward Fletcher to see you."

Lavinia forgot all about the letters lying on the wrought-iron garden table as she leapt to her feet. "I will see him in the drawing room," she told the footman.

"Charlotte! He's here... Reverend Fletcher has arrived. Word has travelled to Cotes Cross of our return."

Lavinia was happy. She had longed to see the vivacious young vicar on many an occasion, since she left for London. She missed seeing his blue eyes sparkle in the sunlight, and she longed to hear his voice. She thought of the way her heart fluttered when she was in his presence, and now that he had come to see her, she could not contain her happiness. In the company of Charlotte, she made her way along the neatly trimmed boxwoods and lush blooms of the garden but resisted the urge to bolt through the door of the house and to run to the drawing room in a very improper manner.

"Miss Talridge! What a delight to see you again after a long season!" he greeted her with a warmth she did not expect from the man she had left in winter.

"Lavinia, I have rung for tea. Is this not a wonderful surprise?" Mrs Talridge asked from her favourite chair in the drawing room, as Reverend Fletcher greeted Charlotte also.

"A surprise?" Lavinia repeated as she noted the gleam in her grandmother's eye. She did not for a moment suspect that her grandmother was surprised by the vicar arriving at her house the day after they had arrived back from London. Lavinia could not be sure, but she had a suspicion that a note had been dispatched early that morning from the desk of the formidable woman. For what reason Lavinia could not ascertain, but she was glad to see a man she hastened to call more than a friend.

"I do not wish to trouble you Mrs Talridge. I came to speak with your granddaughter, and I wonder if I may have permission to take advantage of the air in the garden with her? I have often modelled the garden at the rectory on the success of your design here at Claxton Hall... I might avail myself of it once more in the company of Miss Talridge?"

Mrs Talridge beamed as she replied, "Of course, Lavinia would be delighted to escort you through the garden while Charlotte and I have our tea."

Lavinia was delighted, and she did not question the vicar's interest in the garden or the landscaping of the Hall, as it was famous for its roses and the Tudor knots created from living boxwood. Whether he had come to see the garden or her, she did not care in the least – he was here, and she was glad to be in his company.

"Charlotte and I have just returned from the garden, but I will enjoy accompanying you on a stroll along the paths if you wish. You have to tell me all about the villagers of Cotes Cross and if they are quite well after their bout of illness in the spring?" Lavinia asked as she gazed at the blond curls and blue eyes of the vicar. Today, even in his austere black suit, he seemed to be far bolder than she recalled, and she found him pleasing to gaze upon, at her side. Was it the weather that agreed with him, or was it the absence of many months that put her in the frame of mind to see him so much more favourably?

"If it pleases you Miss Talridge, I do not want to be the cause of your overexertion. We can remain indoors if you would like," he said as they reached the stone steps leading down to the garden.

The scent of the honeysuckle creeping along the stone wall was a heady and inviting scent, as romantic as any rose, Lavinia mused as she inhaled it to calm her nerves, which were in a state. How thrilled she was to be walking at the vicar's side and how transformed he was from his usual reserved nature. His smile was wider, his eyes brighter, and he was wearing his best coat; the one he reserved for dinners and Sundays. With a glance towards his shoes, she saw the glint of polish. He was well turned out, and she wondered what the reason was, as she led him towards the fountain, which was the focal point of the garden for most visitors to Claxton Hall.

"What brings you to the Hall, today Reverend Fletcher?" Lavinia asked as she studied him.

"I received word that you were home from London. I came to welcome you and your grandmother back to Cotes Cross."

"Am I to believe that it was happenstance that brought you to our door on this day?"

"No," he answered, "I do not wish to report of deception, but your grandmother did send a message."

"I suspected that she was the one behind your arrival, although I do not mean to imply that I should not have welcomed it... I wonder what her motive might have been."

"Does there need to be a motive for your parish vicar to call upon you and your family, to see to your health?"

Lavinia giggled, "No, there does not have to be a motive, and as you can see, we are in good health – fine and fit as ever. Tell me of the villagers. You wrote that you were unable to visit us in London because of sickness?"

"Yes, there was bout of influenza, but we were spared the worst of it by God's grace. I am flattered that you noticed my absence from London, but I am sure you must surely have been besieged by eligible gentlemen at every turn, were you not?"

Lavinia stared at her companion, as she replied, "I did not think that you showed the slightest concern for my prospects in London."

"That is where you are wrong, Miss Talridge."

At the fountain, Reverend Fletcher stopped, where the water gushed from the top of the Grecian statue into the stone clamshell underneath. The water sparkled, matching Reverend Fletcher's blue eyes as he looked at Lavinia. There was an expression on his face that she did not recognise. He looked at her with a tenderness that made her pulse race, however there was also a sternness and seriousness in his eyes that made her wonder what the cause could be.

"I have known you for a long time, and you have never once spoken to me of anything other than parish matters, the state of the villagers, and the need for food and medicine in Cotes Cross," Lavinia said.

"If I have kept my distance, it is because I have observed the distance between us in rank and property. That I did not speak of it, until now, does not mean that I was not observant of your prospects. I did not wish to say anything that may have been misconstrued until I discovered how you fared in your season in London. Since you have returned, and I have not been told of any announcement of a fortuitous meeting, or that you are engaged, I may dispense with any hesitation regarding my intentions."

Reverend Fletcher stood close to her – he was so near that she could have reached out and touched his face if she so chose, but she kept her hands clutched nervously together. She was confused by the alteration in his nature and found him to be impassioned in his words and exuberant in a way she had never observed before. However, it was not only his actions that were not clear to her, but also his words.

"What intentions are you implying? I do not understand you, Reverend Fletcher. I am a simple woman, speak plainly to me."

"Have you not ascertained my intentions? I waited for you to go to London, as I did not wish to hamper your efforts if you were to succeed in securing a match with a man of title and influence. Patiently, I tended to my flock until I might hear the news of your marriage. You are home with no such understanding, and I think you might have divined my reason for coming here this day. I have respected you and held you in my highest esteem... unless I am greatly mistaken, you hold me in similar regard."

The breeze that was warm, suddenly felt hot.

The air that held the scent of summer flowers was suddenly stifling with their aroma.

Lavinia was unable to breathe properly, and her chest heaved as she watched Reverend Fletcher reach for her gloved hand. It was the first act of tenderness he had ever shown her. How long had she dreamt of this moment. How many hours had she spent at his side, wishing he would gaze at her with an emotion that was deeper than friendship?

"Miss Talridge, I wish to declare my feelings for you," he said softly. "I have no doubt that your grandmother will be satisfied with my offer of marriage, as there is much to recommend me. I am a respectable member of clergy and well regarded by the finest families in Yorkshire, and if you would accept my proposal, we can be wed by Michaelmas."

Lavinia stared at her hand in his, feeling the gentle but strong grip of his hand. He was asking to marry her. This was all happening so quickly, that she had not the time to consider her answer. Why did she need to consider what her answer would be? She had wanted to be his wife, since the day she had met him, so why was she hesitating?

"Reverend Fletcher, I am flattered by your regard for me."

He laughed.

"I can see that I have given you a shock. Shall we leave the garden and join the others in the drawing room to tell your grandmother and Miss Fenwick the happy news?"

"We should return to the drawing room, but I must confess that I need time to consider your proposal," Lavinia answered in a whisper.

"I understand you feel overwhelmed. I hope it is with happiness, as am I." He said smilingly. "I shall give you all the time that you require. When you have given my proposal every consideration, you shall see that we are a good match, you and I. Imagine the good works we can do in Cotes Cross, the benefit to the villagers, and the reception of our neighbours upon our marriage?" Reverend Fletcher said as he kissed her hand.

She was not accustomed to such forward behaviour from any man, however, Reverend Fletcher was the vicar and not a stranger. She had enjoyed countless hours in his presence and at his side as they endeavoured to help the villagers of Cotes Cross. A kiss on the hand could hardly be improper, and that was the least of her concerns.

Her heart leapt with gladness.

She would say yes.

Surely, she should say it now, but there was something about the quickness of his proposal that made her... uneasy. She cared for the vicar, but did she still love him as she once thought she had? For that reason, she could not say yes immediately, even as she dreamed of a wedding in late September.

Chapter 19

"A proposal of marriage? From Reverend Fletcher?" Major Keeling stated as they walked side by side along the lane to Cotes Cross.

Lavinia did not intend to state her news so bluntly, but she was perplexed about what to do about the vicar. Since becoming friends with him, she had come to rely on Major Keeling's opinion, which was something that would have been disturbing to her a few months ago. She had considered Reverend Fletcher's proposal, carefully guarding it amongst herself and the people she held dear at Claxton Hall. She had not spoken of it to Major Keeling, until this afternoon, when she felt compelled to voice her concerns. He seemed astonished by the news, but his astonishment might have been nothing more than exhaustion, as he had just returned from a journey to London.

Along the lane, in the golden sunshine of the day, Charlotte walked behind Lavinia at a distance. She was acting as a chaperone, but she was not actively part of the conversation. Lavinia knew her friend was hearing every word and would give her opinion later when they were alone. Charlotte was not as opposed to Lavinia's friendship with Major Keeling as Mrs Talridge was, but that may have been because Charlotte was tender-hearted and never held a grudge for too long.

Major Keeling had treated Mrs Talridge with kindness, Charlotte with respect, and he acted towards Lavinia as if they were old and dear friends. The transformation was so complete that Lavinia found herself questioning if she had ever known Major Keeling at all. Since becoming an officer, he was a changed man. He was attentive to her opinions, he laughed with her, and often strolled along the lanes of Cotes Cross in her and Charlotte's company.

"It seems odd to me that he should propose now?" Lavinia said as a farmer slowly approached them in a cart led by a horse.

The cart stopped, and the farmer tipped his ragged hat at the ladies and Major Keeling. "Good day to you ladies, and to you, sir. Thank you for the stew and pudding. We thank you."

Major Keeling replied to the man, "Has your wife's health improved, Mr Pringle?"

"Thank the Lord. We've had a time of it, but she is not as poorly as she was."

"I am glad of it, good day to you."

"Good day to you sir... misses," the farmer said as he made a clicking sound with his mouth and went off at the slow pace of his horse.

Lavinia glanced at Charlotte as she spoke, "You know the farmer, Mr Pringle and his family?"

"We have recently become better acquainted," Major Keeling replied as he changed the subject. "The proposal... have you given an answer yet?"

"I have not, but I do not deny that I should like to say yes."

Major Keeling walked in silence for a few moments. "Why haven't you said yes to Reverend Fletcher yet, if that is what you wish?"

Sighing, Lavinia spoke with honesty. "May I disclose why I have not? You were right to warn me of the opportunists and fortune seekers in London. I would have fallen prey to their deceptions, if it were not for your warnings and my grandmother's insistence that she discover all manner of detail about their backgrounds. I fear that all of my past experiences may have influenced my ability to decide for myself what the best course of action would be. I do not wish to discuss our past, but my wedding day *has,* in a way, affected me... I fear, not in a way that is to my credit."

Major Keeling suddenly seemed to be as distant as the hills far away along the horizon, and Lavinia regretted what she had said, as soon as she noticed his reaction. "Major Keeling, please forgive me if I have offended you. I did not intend to slight you in any way. Since we have become reacquainted, we have spoken to each other as honestly as old friends. I do not want to renew any painful feelings from the past."

"There is no need for you to apologise for offending me. I have striven with all my effort to earn your good opinion of me, but I know that it will not erase the wrongs of our history. If your words caused me any discomfort, it was from the knowledge of my own actions."

As they strolled side by side along the road, a quiet hung over them, and Lavinia hoped that the silence was not a sign that anything was amiss. She enjoyed being with Major Keeling in a way that she had not, when they were engaged, and she found comfort in it. She had enjoyed speaking her mind, until that moment. He was upset, and she had said too much. She wished she could withdraw her statement, but the damage was done.

As they entered Cotes Cross, Major Keeling remarked, "Did the vicar make his feelings for you known when you arrived home to Claxton Hall?"

"Yes, he came to see me the day after we arrived."

"I wonder why he did not apprise you of his intentions while he was in London."

"London?" Lavinia was surprised. "He never was in London. He wished to go to town, but he wrote to me that he was unable to pay a visit because the village of Cotes Cross was stricken with influenza."

His green eyes flashed as he looked at her, and a quizzical expression came over his face. "He wrote to you that he did not journey to London."

"He did sir. I was rather disappointed," Lavinia said quickly.

"How strange then, that I should have observed him in London before I returned to Cotes Cross..."

"Perhaps you were mistaken? London is a large place filled with a great many people."

"Perhaps you are right, Miss Talridge. I may be mistaken, but I do think you are wise to not be too hasty in your answer to his proposal."

Lavinia did not know what to make of Major Keeling's warning, nor his observation of Reverend Fletcher in London. London was enormous, that was true, but she was sure that the vicar must look like many young men his age.

Chapter 20

The month of June was a memory, and July was nearly half over, when Lavinia realised that she had not yet given an answer to the vicar. Not only had she not given him an answer, but she knew that her grandmother was growing impatient. Mrs Talridge made her feelings known early one morning after breakfast, when Lavinia found herself summoned to the study – her grandmothers' private room. The dark and foreboding room housed all the papers and books related to the running of the estate, all of her correspondence, and her personal library. Being in the room was like being in the very heart of Claxton Hall and the immense land it occupied. Maps sat rolled on the shelves. Bookcases lined the walls behind locked glass doors. These cases were filled with ledgers and every manner of book or paper that Mrs Talridge required to oversee all of her accounts, which were numerous. Lavinia was not a child, but in the presence of her grandmother, who was seated at her dark oak desk, she felt as if she had been disobedient.

"I can see that you are occupied but know that you have a wish to speak with me. If I may, I would like to make a request that I am sure you will not find objectionable," Lavinia said as she concentrated very hard on keeping her voice steady. There was something in the way her grandmother looked at her, which seemed to indicate that she was displeased with Lavinia.

With a steely look, Mrs Talridge replied, "Yes, there is a matter of the utmost importance that we need to settle, but I suppose it can wait until you have divulged this request. Although I should mention that you are in no position to request anything after your behavior this summer."

Dreading the conversation that was to come, Lavinia plunged ahead, fearing that she had picked a poor time to ask for anything. But she told herself, this was not for her, but for woman whom she held dear. With a steely resolve, she said, "It's about Charlotte. She wants to be married, to be settled with a husband. We have more than enough money to sustain us, the estate, and the whole village of Cotes Cross. This may not the best time to ask this, but I wish to set a dowry and annuity for her as a token of my, of our, appreciation for her years of selfless companionship."

Mrs Talridge's expression softened as she answered, "I was not expecting you to say that. I have thought of giving her such a gift if she should become engaged. She has never mentioned a gentleman of interest to me – is there someone she wishes to marry?"

"Captain Sutherland."

"My, that would be an ambitious match on her part. I have no doubt his family would prefer a duchess, but if her dowry was generous, and she was well connected, then I can see no reason for their objection."

"Would you give her a dowry of her own... would you give her a reference?" Lavinia asked expectedly.

"I am astonished that you even have to ask. Consider it done. I shall see to it. I am pleased that she has shown herself to be an example to you. She wishes to marry, which leads me to the very reason why I called you in here, Lavinia. As we are alone, I do not have to remind you that you are taking advantage of the patience of a perfectly respectable gentleman who has asked for your hand in marriage," Mrs Talridge said from her seat behind the desk.

Lavinia shifted uncomfortably in the wooden chair, wishing to be anywhere else but in the study. She looked out the window at the haze on the lawn, where a mist was swirling above the green grass – an inviting picture, and one which distracted her from her grandmother's scowling face.

"Lavinia! Pay attention! You told Reverend Fletcher that you would give every consideration to his offer. That was a month ago and yet you have still not accepted? This is scandalous. I should warn you that rumours of your upcoming wedding have reached my ears from our society here in Yorkshire and yesterday I was asked when the happy date was, by Sir Applegate's wife no less. I ask you what is the meaning of this? If you do not make an announcement soon, there will be talk and I dread to think what shall be said!"

"Not this again. There was talk after Major Keeling abandoned me on our wedding day. Am I to endure gossip at every juncture of my life?"

"Until you are married and respectable as a wife, yes, you will have no choice but to endure rumours and conjecture. The other choice is to remain unwed, but that will never do. As the sole heiress of Claxton Hall, you *must* marry in order to preserve the lineage." She tried to calm down. "Enough talk about rumours... what are you going to do? Reverend Fletcher has been the epitome of patience, and his interest was expressed to you and to me quite clearly. I cannot find fault with the match, even if I would have wished you a gentleman with higher rank or at the very least, a title."

"What of his circumstances?"

"What of his circumstances? Vicars and members of the clergy are not often wealthy. If they were wealthy, they would seek other occupations or none at all."

Lavinia pursed her lips, a habit that plagued her when she concentrated very hard upon a subject. She knew her grandmother expected an answer, and it was only right that she and Reverend Fletcher be given a reason for Lavinia's reticence.

"Lavinia, you have not given me a reason why you should not come to a decision, so tell me... what is there to decide? You are not young, your season in London did not go as well as I would have liked, and here you sit, with a proposal from a man whom you know well and admire – and you have done nothing about it. If you remain unwed after *this*, you shall have a reputation that will not serve you."

"Are you implying that Reverend Fletcher may be my very last hope for finding a husband?"

Lavinia's grandmother seemed angered by her comment.

"I mean that he may be your last hope for finding a husband who is not marrying you *for* Claxton Hall. I have had my fill of those gold diggers in London and never have I seen so promising a parade of gentlemen amount to little more than gamblers and penniless lords."

"Then I should make haste to accept Reverend Fletcher?"

"Why have you not done so already? Why have you hesitated? Are you waiting for some other gentleman to propose, or do you have a secret you're hiding from me?"

"A secret? When have I ever had secrets from you? You are my grandmother and I know you mean well by all that you do for me," Lavinia answered, despite feeling the guilt that comes from a lie.

She *did* have a secret.

She was ashamed to admit it to herself, and to say it would make it true, but she dared not confess it.

"Shall we invite Reverend Fletcher for dinner so that you may tell him the happy news that he will become your husband?" her grandmother asked impatiently. "May we make the announcement?"

"Invite him to dinner, grandmother, yes, that would be nice. We shall have cook make his favoured dishes."

"Now you're thinking like a wife and the future mistress of Claxton Hall," Mrs Talridge said, relieved, and with a proudness in her voice that Lavinia had not often heard.

Lavinia smiled at her grandmother, as the older woman handed her a small stack of letters to post. She was being dismissed, her fate and her life decided in one conversation.

The vicar was a handsome man. He was charming, and he cared for the villagers of Cotes Cross. More than that, he seemed to hold her in his regard.

After all, she *did* like the vicar, and she would be proud to become his wife.

But love?

The love she had once felt for him could possibly reignite into a feeling that would sustain her for many years of marriage.

But had it been love, or only a childish affection for a man who was both good-looking and who embodied the ideal of everything she thought she wanted in a husband?

With a wave to Charlotte who was in the drawing room attending to her favourite pastime of embroidery, Lavinia placed the letters on a table by the door, and left Claxton Hall without a bonnet or her gloves. In the early morning, she did not think anyone would see her along the lane except for the occasional farmer or some other person from the village with whom she was well acquainted. This was not London, and she was not concerned with impressing anyone she might meet at that moment. With her future well in hand, she felt constrained and confined, even as she breathed in the crisp morning air.

Now that the decision had been made, and she had accepted what felt to be inevitable, she did not feel joy. The secret that her grandmother had guessed she was hiding, were her feelings for another man. As she walked along the dirty road leading away from Claxton Hall, she sighed, and then she sighed again, enjoying the freedom of expressing herself without shocking Miss Fenwick or disturbing her grandmother. There was no footman to observe her, or maid to sneak down the servant's stairs to tell the other maids how badly Lavinia was behaving. She was outside, and she was free, at least for the present. When she became the vicar's wife, she would no longer be free. When she became the mistress of Claxton Hall, she would have to wear a bonnet and gloves and attend to the estate.

The responsibilities of her future life weighed heavily, as she kicked at a dirt clod along the road, in frustration. Why did the prospect of marrying Mr Keeling before he was the major, feel less like a trap than marrying a man such as Reverend Fletcher, whom she adored in most ways and found to be agreeable company? Why was she thinking about Major Keeling at all? He had become a noble character, his honour had been restored, and he was redeemed in her view of him, which was, as with her feelings for him, unexpected. Could she be in love with him?

"No", she said aloud to the cold misty air. "Oh... no!" she said again. How could she allow herself to love a man who had disappointed her in the past? But was he still that man? *No*, she whispered as she thought about him. It was strange that knowing him as a major made her feel as if she had met him for the first time. This man she knew, the one who had returned from war, was a different man. He was a man of his word, he saw to the needs of the villagers and the farmers, he had reconciled with his father and with her, and he was changed in nearly every other way that mattered. Yes, she was in love with Major Keeling – but that should not have to matter, because she was going to marry the vicar... the decision had been made. *Besides*, she thought, *Major Keeling had not sought her hand, nor had he offered the slightest indication that he wished to do so* – actually he had done quite the opposite... She knew that in September she would become the happy wife of the vicar and that her life was therefore planned and sealed, just like a letter.

Letters! She had forgotten to post her grandmother's letters! She knew the woman would be furious, so Lavinia turned around and rushed back to the house. Lifting her skirt (quite unlady-like) to run faster, she was nearly at the Hall when she heard the thundering of horses' hooves along the road.

Dropping her skirt and smoothing the wrinkles and dust from it, she reached up to her hair, and recalled that she was without a bonnet. It was too late to worry about that now, as the rider was approaching so quickly that Lavinia hastened to step off the road onto the wet grass to avoid being struck.

"Whoa!" The man said in the mist as the horse reared up, landing on its front hooves near Lavinia and giving her a scare.

"Sir! Take care!" she called out as she looked up at the rider of the horse.

"Miss Talridge, is that you on the road? I could have killed you!" Major Keeling said, as he jumped down from his steed.

"And so you nearly did," she said, shaking.

"Are you hurt? Is anything amiss?" He reached for her hand, a gesture she found as touching as it was unexpected.

"I am not hurt... startled yes, but not injured. Where did you come from at such a rate of speed? I was just thinking about..." she started to say, before hastily realising that in her scared state she had nearly spoken the truth and admitted that she had been thinking about him.

"I came from Brigham Park. I have been in London on business, and then I journeyed to Manchester, but my itinerary is not of importance."

Major Keeling's hands rested on Lavinia's shoulders, and his face was close to hers, his green eyes peering at her as he spoke. "Tell me, you haven't entered into an engagement with Reverend Fletcher yet, have you?"

Lavinia searched his face for any sign of why he demanded such an answer. "Why are you asking, Mr Keeling?"

"Then you have agreed to marry him, but you are not yet wed?" he said as he lowered his hands and reached for the reins of his horse.

"I am not yet wed, and I have not agreed to marry him, although my grandmother has made the decision for me. She says that Cotes Cross expects a wedding."

"Cotes Cross is talking about you and the vicar, but they have been talking about that since June. I have news, terribly distressing news, that I am afraid I must tell you."

"Distressing news? About him?"

"Yes, Miss Talridge, and you may feel mournful and despairing when I impart to you what I have discovered," he said as he stared at her, his gaze unwavering.

"We should go into the house if I am to hear terrible news... I do not think the lane is the place for such a pronouncement."

A quarter of an hour later, Lavinia sat on the edge of the couch in the drawing room. Charlotte was seated nearby, and Mrs Talridge sat in her customary place, a frown fixed to her face as she surveyed Major Keeling. Major Keeling looked exhausted, as though he had not slept. His coat was wrinkled, and his boots were dirty.

He cleared his throat.

With his head bowed low under the weight of the news he was to impart, he breathed in deeply and then with his usual confidence, looked at Lavinia, his gaze as unwavering as it had been on the lane.

"Major Keeling, if you won't share the news that you have chosen to relay in such a dramatic fashion, with my granddaughter, then I have correspondence that requires my immediate attention," Mrs Talridge said, as she glared at him.

"Very well," Major Keeling began as he addressed the small group of women, all of whom were sitting in rapt attention. He spoke slowly and deliberately. "Mrs Talridge, Miss Talridge, and Miss Fenwick, I do not wish to be the messenger of ill tidings and bad news, but I must do my duty. As Miss Talridge is aware, in London, I vowed to be her protector and champion, and a guardian against all manner of evil that may befall her. It was my attempt to make amends to her and to you, Mrs Talridge, after the harm I caused to your family in my youth. It is with this intention that I communicate what I have discovered to be the truth about an acquaintance you hold dear."

Lavinia was anxious, "Tell us quickly, as I cannot abide the suspense of not knowing what has caused you to ride as if you had no need of sleep."

"I have not slept as I changed horses at Brigham Park and came here from Manchester. It is the news I learned in that fair city which hastened my arrival, so forgive me for the state of my appearance."

"Yes, yes, you are forgiven, now what is this news?" Mrs Talridge demanded.

"The news, if I may state it with delicacy, concerns Mr Fletcher."

"Reverend Fletcher?" Miss Fenwick asked, her own pretty brow furrowed from concern. "The vicar?"

"The very one," he spoke to Miss Fenwick and then turned his attention to Lavinia as he addressed her. "I learned of his proposal this summer, as you recall, Miss Talridge. I was struck by the strangeness of the timing of it, since he had proposed after the change in your fortunes. When I met him, after I came home from the war, I realised that I had seen him before, in London. There is no polite way to explain where I saw him and in whose company, so I shall speak plainly – I saw him in the clubs where men gamble. He had lost a fortune in a single night. He was accompanied by several men who I knew to be opportunists and card sharps. I learned from Captain Sutherland that he, the vicar, was a man of many dissolute habits and prone to gambling, drinking, and to frequenting establishments, the names of which I shall not mention."

"He is a member of the clergy." Lavinia said as she tried to make sense of what she was hearing. "Where would he obtain the money to gamble? You say he lost a small fortune?"

"Captain Sutherland did not know, but he presumed the money lost was either the last of Mr Fletcher's inheritance or money from the coffers of his parish," explained Major Keeling.

"Sir, you have *no* evidence of the slanderous charges you have brought against a gentleman who shall be married to my granddaughter." Mrs Talridge waved her fan indignantly. "*Reverend* Fletcher is known to be a man of honour who has served this village and this county. How *dare* you speak against him?" She jumped to her feet, her eyes blazing with anger.

"I have proof, Mrs Talridge." Major Keeling said calmly. "I have come to news from Captain Sutherland of a crime far worse than the habits I have reported. Mr Fletcher, the very same vicar who serves in this parish, was forced to leave Manchester after attempting to elope with the daughter of a magistrate." Mrs Talridge opened her mouth in shock and dropped the fan as Major Keeling continued. "Although the woman in question was not a titled lady, her father was quite wealthy and her dowry considerable. They were found at an inn, *The Red Hart*, on the way to Scotland, to Gretna Green."

Charlotte gasped, "Gretna Green? The village that allows people to marry without a proper church announcement?"

"The very same one. The young woman's reputation was irreversibly ruined, and Mr Fletcher had to re-establish himself here in Yorkshire. He is a fortune hunter who owes gambling debts to men who are far too terrible to mention in the presence of ladies."

Mrs Talridge stared at Major Keeling.

"I have proof of that, too."

Mrs Talridge and Charlotte were speechless, as Lavinia felt nauseous and giddy at the same time. Was it possible that once again she had chosen poorly when it came to matrimony? Charlotte, who had noticed her displeasure, tried to cheer her up with comforting words. "Lavinia, do not grieve. You can be thankful! You have managed to avoid an unhappy marriage through fate."

Major Keeling met Mrs Talridge's glare as he said, "Mrs Talridge, I know you are a woman of resources. I have evidence, but you may wish to have these charges investigated. In fact, I would prefer that you learn independently that what I say is true. You may rely on my discretion, until such time as you have conducted your own research into the scoundrel's background. It is not my wish to ruin a man's reputation, unnecessarily, but if he insists on preying upon Miss Talridge, I may be forced to do so. There are numerous men in London who wish to know of his whereabouts, as well as the magistrate who warned him against seeking out other unsuspecting women."

Mrs Talridge plopped back into her chair and shook her head. She sighed. "If what you say *is* true, and of course I have reason at present to doubt you, what cause do you have for taking it upon yourself to uncover the truth about Reverend Fletcher? What do you wish to gain?" Mrs Talridge demanded. "Surely you do not wish to see my granddaughter become a spinster?"

"No, I do not wish so – I want to see her happily married to a man who deserves her, who loves her, and who will stop at nothing to protect her from every harm," he said, reaching for Lavinia's hand, as he spoke.

Lavinia had been reeling from the news about Reverend Fletcher but found herself recovered as soon as Major Keeling touched her. Time slowed in the drawing room as she allowed him to hold her hand, and asked, "Who are you referring to when you say those things? What man can there be who loves me, and who cares for me and not my fortune?"

"I am that man who would happily marry you and love you." His eyes sparkled as he looked into hers. "I love you Miss Talridge. I love you and I do not deserve your hand in marriage, but I will ask for it with all my heart."

Lavinia stared at him, too shocked to say anything.

She wanted to say yes, to agree to marry him, to... but her grandmother suddenly raised her voice. "Unhand her! Who are you but the penniless second son of a viscount? You have become no better than a fortune hunter. How scandalous to think the village expects a wedding between the vicar and my granddaughter, and they will have one between you and her instead?"

"Mrs Talridge, I may be the second son of a viscount, but I am not penniless."

"How have your fortunes changed? I thought you were resigned to live on your army pension?" Lavinia whispered without removing her hand from his.

"Upon our reconciliation, my father provided me with a small allowance. With that allowance I wisely invested in Captain Sutherland's newest venture and I am now an investor in the tea exporting business, which has already reaped a tidy profit. I have no reason to suspect that my fortune will decrease. It would be monstrous if I were to ask for your hand in marriage, Miss Talridge, if I had no means with which to increase the wealth of Claxton Hall – that is why I have not spoken up before." Again, facing Mrs Talridge, he continued, "I was born Mr George Keeling, the second son of a Viscount, but the support of General Wellington and the generosity of our prince regent gave me a knighthood and made me Sir Keeling. Property bought with the profits of my investment might not be as grand as Claxton Hall, but I will aspire to become a worthy member of Yorkshires gentry. Lavinia should become a Duchess and have all that life has to offer, but I would be the happiest of men, if I could call her my Lady Keeling."

"Major Keeling..." Mrs Talridge's voice was suddenly much calmer again, "your circumstances have undoubtedly changed." She paused, "If... what you have told us is true, then what assurance does my granddaughter have that you will not abandon her again? Why should she trust you? Why should we all trust you?" she asked as Charlotte stared in wide-eyed astonishment. Mrs Talridge's eyes, too, were stubbornly focused on Major Keeling.

Only Lavinia gazed relaxed and happy at the man who she knew she loved, as if she were in a dream.

"He does not have to give assurances or promises. I love him, and he loves me," Lavinia spoke, her voice loud and clear. "He has done everything in his power to prove that he is worthy of my trust and my respect since that day at Lady Whitfield's."

"What of our neighbours?" asked Mrs Talridge.

"What of them? The village wants a wedding, so we will let them have one," the major sounded amused.

"What of the Reverend ... of Mr Fletcher?" Mrs Talridge asked.

"If he seeks a fortune, he may seek it elsewhere. I am not hurt by him, but I am shocked that I did not uncover the truth for myself. Thank you, Major Keeling, for being my champion," Lavinia said as she rose to her feet, her hand in his.

"Charlotte my dear," Mrs Talridge motioned to Miss Fenwick, and they rushed from the drawing room.

Lavinia and Major Keeling were alone.

"Do you forgive me, for all that I have done? Will you have me for your husband?" he said as he knelt before her.

"There is nothing to forgive. You have redeemed yourself in more than one way."

"You agree to become my wife?"

"You must not leave me on my wedding day, not again, or I shall never forgive you."

"You have my word as an officer, that that shall never happen and this time I will never leave your side."

"There is one other vow I wish to hear before you have my decision," Lavinia said as she became lost in his eyes.

"Yes, my dearest. What is that vow, I will take it."

"When we are married, I wish to be wed at Brigham Park, in the chapel. That was the first night I saw who you were, the real George Keeling. That night I could have fallen in love with you."

"Yes, we can be wed at the chapel if you wish. It would make me very happy to see you at that altar by my side."

Breathlessly, Lavinia whispered her answer, "You may have my answer. Yes... I will marry you."

"You have no concern for the scandal this will cause, and that you will be married to a man who is in trade?"

"If you don't mind being married to the daughter of a village seamstress," Lavinia asked, hesitantly. Did he know that she was not only born poor, but also out of wedlock? Haltingly, she said, "and born outside of the bonds of matrimony."

His gaze was steady and unwavering as he allayed her fears, "I love you for all that you are. I love you as the poor village girl and heiress... Oh, Lavinia, I have known the truth of your birth for as long as I've known you. It has done nothing to diminish my regard for you. Say that you will become my wife, and I shall always love you."

Lavinia wanted to cry tears of jubilation and relief as she said, "I love you too, for the brash young aristocrat and the man I see before me today, for the conceited youth and the major."

Lavinia could not see anything else but the intensely penetrating gaze of her future husband's green eyes as they leaned in close to each other. His eyes shone with a hunger that made her weak with longing. There was a tension that rippled between them like a coming storm. With a gentle sweetness, closely followed by delicious urgency, Major Keeling's lips touched hers, tenderly at first but then impatiently. She was swept away in the moment, lost in the mesmerizing feeling of his kiss. His strong arms, thick and muscled, held her as delicately as if she were priceless. His scent, so clean and masculine, incited a passion deep within her. How long had she desired to be in his arms, to hear the words he spoke, telling her that he loved her? How many nights had she dreamt of his lips on hers, of a feeling so timeless and strong that she wished it would never end? Surrendering to his kiss, his heart beating next to hers as he held her, she no longer felt trapped by her future.

In the embrace of the man she loved, the man she would love for all eternity – she felt free.

The End

Dear Reader,

Did you enjoy my romance novel? If you did, I'd love to invite you to read my next book titled "The Duke of the Moors." Miss Catherine Conolly is surprised by an invitation from a wealthy uncle who hasn't spoken to her in years. Upon arriving at his formidable house on the Yorkshire Moors, she finds herself a pawn in his mischievous plan to gain influence over the enigmatic Duke of Rotherham – known as the

Duke of the Moors. But enthralling as she finds the handsome man, his reputation and inscrutable manner are the subjects of much sinister speculation among the locals and the society crowd alike ...

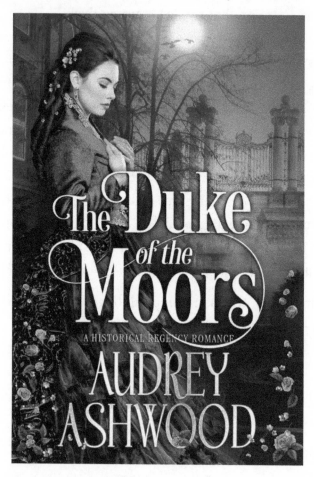

Would you like to be informed as soon as the next volume in the series is published? If so, then sign up here to my mailing list: www.audreyashwood.com/releases.

Yours,

Audrey Ashwood

The Author

Audrey Ashwood

Author of Clean Historical Romance

Audrey Ashwood hails from London, the city where she was born and raised. At a young age, she began diving into the world of literature, a world full of fairytales and Prince Charmings. Writing came later – no longer was she a spectator of fantasies; she was now a creator of them.

In her books, the villains get their just desserts – her stories are known for happy and deserved endings. Love, of course, plays a major role, even if it's not the initial star of the show. With each written word, Audrey hopes to remind people that love transcends oceans and generations.

Don't miss out on exciting offers and new releases.

Sign up for her newsletter and the exclusive Reader's Circle: www.audreyashwood.com/releases

Legal Information

A Bride for the Viscount's Cold Son;
A Regency Romance Novel
by Audrey Ashwood;

Published by:
ARP 5519, 1732 1st Ave #25519 New York, NY 10128
January 2019
Contact: info@allromancepublishing.com

1. Edition Paperback (Version 1.2); January 1st, 2019
© 2019

Image Rights:

© Period Images
© Depositphotos.com

Updated November 1st, 2019